Acclaim for

ANDREW LAFLECHE

"Andrew Lafleche is an honest and courageous writer. There is an eyes-wide-open accuracy to his work, no matter the subject matter. Hemingway once said of writers he admired: 'They're true gen,' meaning they were the genuine article, writers he considered incapable of deceit, and incapable of playing dumb. Andrew is a True Gen writer."

—Ron Corbett, award-winning journalist, broadcaster
and author of the Frank Yakabuski crime novels

"He's like a surgeon with a shotgun."

—Akeem Duncan, *Quiet Lunch Magazine*

"The memories kicked up by this trip lead Troy on a bender of extreme and violent proportions—he robs drug dealers, ruins friendships, and fills his system with whatever chemicals he can. As he self-destructs, he tells himself to just "enjoy the ride," but that may be because he doesn't realize the dark places that the ride will take him. Lafleche tells the story in Troy's own voice—a caustic blend of casual slurs, teenage id, and affected nihilism—and the novel as a whole fits very well within the tradition of transgressive literature."

—*Kirkus Reviews*

"Andrew Lafleche's *Ride*, like a sharp new switchblade, has a dangerous weight to it. Troy accidentally stabs his friend, his parents are divorcing, he's high risk with sex, drugs, and crime, and he's giving his life the finger. *Ride* is highway speed and echoes Irvine Welsh's *Trainspotting*, only with Canadian accents."

—Gerald Arthur Moore, author
of *Shatter the Glass, Shards of Flame*

"I laughed. I cried. I cringed."

—Karen Connelly, author of *The Change Room*

"Lafleche's *Ride* is a fast paced binge in a style that resembles early American detective fiction like Mickey Spillane's. Dialogue is terse, punch-rough and trade-sex-ready as the action explodes like gas on a fire. The main character, Troy, tries to douse his own burning desires with beer, sex and drugs, only to feel raw regret each morning. The things he does, or fails to do, are like melted beer cans among the ashes of morning—and he hasn't seen his shrink in days. 'I am nobody, who knows nothing,' Leary's third generation 'turned on, tuned in, and dropping out' as Lafleche weaves a counterculture of loathing that mirrors a Hunter S. Thompson circus party. This is a bush party in the heart of the city, and in the heart of Troy. The question is: will he survive?"

—Keith Inman, author of *The War Poems* and *SEAsya*

Andrew Lafleche

RIDE

ANDREW LAFLECHE is an award-winning poet and the author of *Ashes, No Diplomacy, Shameless, A Pardonable Offence, One Hundred Little Victories, On Writing, Merica, Merica, on the Wall,* and *After I Turn into Alcohol.* He is editor of Gravitas Poetry. Lafleche holds an M.A. in Creative and Critical Writing from the University of Gloucestershire.
www.AndrewLafleche.com

Books by

ANDREW LAFLECHE

Ashes

No Diplomacy

Shameless

A Pardonable Offence

One Hundred Little Victories

On Writing

Merica, Merica, on the Wall

After I Turn into Alcohol

ENJOY THE

RIDE

Andrew Lafleche

Pub House Books

Montreal

FIRST PUB HOUSE BOOKS EDITION, SEPTEMBER 2020

Portions of this book have previously appeared
in *Voicing Suicide* and *The Bookends Review*.

Library and Archives Canada Cataloguing in Publication

Title: Ride / Andrew Lafleche.
Names: Lafleche, Andrew, author.
Description: First Pub House Books edition.
Identifiers: Canadiana 20200209442 | ISBN 9781989266274 (softcover)
Classification: LCC PS8623.A3582 R53 2020 | DDC C813/.6—dc23

ISBN-13 978-1-989266-27-4

Book design by John Warden

Pub House Books
1918 Boul. Saint-Regis
Dorval, QC H9P 1H6

Printed in the United States of America

For Lucas. Forever.

He told me not to think of him like a psychiatrist and more as a friend in confidence; someone to bounce ideas off. It sounded like a game of ping pong to me.

"This is a safe space," he said. "Everything you share is confidential."

I knew he was lying, and he knew I knew he was a lying. I didn't say a word.

He fiddled with his glasses. "You can be completely honest in here."

Sum 41's "Fat Lip" blared through the headphones that hung around my neck. He never asked me to turn it off or down. I was testing for boundaries. I wanted to make sure he knew how much I disdained being there, that our time together was forced, that I wouldn't participate.

Dr. Dimock stared at his legal pad. He had a habit of tonguing his lips. I scanned the room counting the certificates on the cigarette stained walls. Five to assure whoever sat in my chair that this overweight, sweaty, glasses wearing middle-aged man really was a doctor and I should trust him. If anyone ever tells you it's a safe place and to think of them as your friend the first time you meet, you know it's not a safe place and they are certainly not your friend.

"What brings you in here today?" he asked.

I counted the second hand on the clock. It was math class all over again.

He never looked up at me, just kept asking dumb questions that I wouldn't answer, and scratched at his yellow sheets of paper.

"Who do you think the most famous person in the world is?"

"What?" That one caught me off guard.

"Who do you think the most famous person in the world is?"

I smiled, partly because I like messing with people, partly to see if he was even listening, and partly because it's who everybody seemed to be talking about on the news. "Osama bin Laden."

It was five to five. He scribbled something on his legal pad, looked up for the first time, and asked me what I meant by Osama bin Laden being the most famous person in the world. I told him that I had to get going, pulled my headphones over my ears, and walked out of the office.

My mom was waiting for me outside. She asked how the session went. I told her it was bullshit and made the stonewalling face; a forced blank expression with eyes of rage. "Just give it a chance, Troy," she said.

I snapped, "I can't believe you sold me out like that." The rest of the drive I stared out the window.

When we got home, I went straight to my room, closed the door, turned on the stereo and listened to System of a Down at full volume. Between tracks I could hear my mom sobbing on the phone. I figured she realized I wasn't going back to see Dr. Dimock again.

. . .

My cell rang. It was Ed. He wanted to head over to Virgil and hit the new half-pipe they put in at the arena. I paused to give the appearance of thinking about it. I hated sounding too eager. "Sure," I said.

"Be outside in twenty. Emily'll drive us."

Emily was Ed's girlfriend. She should have been mine. I've known her longer, and I've had a hard crush ever since I first laid eyes on her. Five-foot nothing and blonde hair hanging down between her shoulders. Emily had the soft face of a young girl not yet jaded by men. Her eyes were always lined in dark colours. Purple was my favourite. That's what she had on when we first met. She wore a shy smile. Don't even get me started on her body. The girl is a ten; I don't award those easily either. She smelled like Britney Spears. Well, at least she used Britney Spears' perfume.

It was a football game after school, home opener or spirit week or some other forced fun that allowed us to be excused from last period to attend. Em mentioned she was going and I told her I was too. I don't usually go to those sorts of things, for a girl though, of course. No that's not entirely true, there are some girls I wouldn't go with. I wouldn't go with a Liberated Feminist that's for sure. Well, unless for a quick two pump and dump. I hoped going would somehow lead to her and I getting together.

It was a terrible game, I think. It was cold and starting to rain a bit. Emily wore the thin long sleeve shirt that girls always wear even if they know it's going to be cold outside. It hugged her body in all the right places. I knew she was cold so I offered her my sweater. It was the only name brand sweater I had, a yellow and blue striped Tommy Hilfiger job. It came in a bag of hand-me-downs from one of my older cousins I didn't really know. Name brands were a big thing in high school, that's why I remember it was Tommy Hilfiger. Emily thanked me for the sweater and gave me a hug. If a girl takes your sweater then you're pretty much on route to becoming her boyfriend. At least that's what I thought in those early high school years. After the game she left with her friends and I left with mine and the next day I found out she had started dating this guy named Ed. The fuck? Now that I think of it, I don't think she ever gave me that sweater back, the bitch.

There was a decommissioned railroad track running beside the asphalt that lined the skate park's edge. I pulled out a baggie of cocaine and asked Ed if he wanted to do a rail off the rails. I was being clever.

He nodded over his shoulder. "Not with Emily around."

I glared at him. I hated that he kept things from her. Vulnerability always lies in pretending to be someone you're not.

"Get rid of her then," I said.

She was sitting on the bench, texting, and half watching us as we cursed and bailed and cheered whenever we messed up or landed a trick.

Ed pulled a ten from his pocket and gestured at Emily. "Em, go get us some Gatorade."

He walked over and waved the bill in her face. She sighed, stood up, snatched the bill from him, and marched toward the arena.

"I'm keeping the change," she scoffed.

Ed could be a real douchebag. I don't know why she was with him. It was obvious neither of them was happy. Or at least that's what I always told myself.

After she left, I poured some coke on one of the rails and used a card to cut four lines. I hit one, Ed huffed two, then I snorted the last one before Emily returned with the drinks.

Ed clapped my shoulder grinning. "Rails off rails, bro. Classic."

Emily brought the drinks and asked how long we would be there. "There's a party on Lakeshore," she said.
Ed threw his board down and pumped across the asphalt. "Ten more minutes."

Emily played the new Blink-182 album. The country air poured through the open windows. She shifted the car into third as the stereo blared, "Seventeen without a purpose or direction, we don't owe anyone a fuckin' explanation."

When we arrived at the party, I was jonesing for another line, Ed too, so I found the bathroom, locked the door, and cut four more. That's what I hated about cocaine, its non-lasting qualities. Although this hate wasn't enough to stop me from nostriling it down. I took two off the toilet tank, flushed, and left the room. Ed knew the routine and was waiting outside the door. I walked down the stairs to join the party, half listening for the bathroom door to close and the fan to click on.

The house was filled with a bunch of kids dressed in argyle vests and skinny jeans. One guy had a bull ring pierced through his nose. Another had bottle cap sized discs in his ears. Hair was worn in two styles: straight cut and gelled or, knotted and messy in dreads. The girls added highlighted streaks of purple and green for effect. They all wore thick-framed glasses. None of them were drunk but they seemed to be having a good time anyway. Despite them all looking the same, there were distinct cliques divided by their "I want to be different like everybody else" appearance. I couldn't tell the difference.

This was not my scene.

Outside someone offered me a joint. I took a couple hits and started to cough. My eyes watered and I knew it'd been sprayed with Windex. Some dealers spray their weed with Windex to make it weigh more. I passed it back and the guy said, "Good shit, eh?" I recognized him from school but we'd never talked.

He was a skinny basketball kid who did a lot of speed and was always bouncing around the hallway. Once, I walked into the gym and he was all by himself, hand standing against the wall, pumping off push up after push up. Still, he was a twig. I don't remember what he was like before his brother killed himself, but since then he's been completely strung.

"Got any blow?" he asked me.

"Nah man, just finished the last of it," I lied.

"Shit. Well, if you want to go in on a ball, I got a pretty good hookup."

His brother blew his face off with a shotgun in his bedroom at their family home. Rumour had it that he owed a boatload of cash to the biker's for cocaine and couldn't pay.

I nodded.

He passed me back the joint but I said no thanks and he sort of just walked off with it. One of the other guys in the circle turned to me and said, "You can't give him any blow, dude. He snaps on that stuff. Jase was one of my best friends and I know he'd hate to see his brother get all messed up like he did."

The guy that was talking to me, rumour also had it that he stole the blow from Jase, his best friend. I didn't care either way. Didn't look like he did either. If buddy wanted to get high, let him. I didn't know his brother and barely knew him and it's not really possible to care about someone you don't know.

I spotted Matty across the yard. He was seated by one of those backyard fire chimneys. I gave him a wave, "Hey, Matty."

"Sup, Troy?"

"Thinking about taking off. These people depress me."

"Yeah, I'm just here to drink their beer and then I'll be out too. You want a bump of K?"

He pulled a vile from his pocket. The powder looked like shards of glass. He poured a generous pile on the web of my hand.

"Thanks, dude."

I stiffed the bump and lit a cigarette. There was a trio of girls huddled nearby. I recognized them from school too, but we'd never shared two words. They kind of just watched Matty and me and whispered shit to each other. Whatever, let them talk.

I stepped toward Matty to take a seat and lifted my foot too high; enough to lose my balance and stumbled to the side. Ketamine is a cat tranquilizer. On people it's like funnelling twenty-four beers up the nose. It's a hell of a drug.

"Moon walk, baby," Matty laughed. I recovered and sat down. "Did I show you my new knife?"

"No man," I said. "Let's see it."

He pulled out an automatic switch, flicked it open, and handed it over. It was an Italian job, shiny redwood for the handle, cold stainless steel for the blade. The thing had some weight to it.

"Cool," I said, stabbing the air in front of me. I looked over at Matty, smiled, and pretended to stab him in the leg. He jumped back, "Are you crazy? These are new jeans."

"I wasn't going to cut you, I just wanted to see you fall off your chair. It was a joke." I folded the knife closed and handed it back to him. He passed me a beer.

Sitting in silence, blitzed on K, drunk, high on blow, he told me to give him my hand and then poured me another bump. Sometimes you can hallucinate on the stuff, but we hadn't done nearly enough.

Matty did another bump then looked at his jeans.

"Shit, Troy. I think you got me. My jeans are soaked."

"It's probably beer," I said. "Or you pissed yourself."

"I don't know, man. Flick your lighter at it."

I pulled out my Zippo and snapped the cap open lit. It was a trick I learned that cost too many hours practising not to show off. Under the flame there was a circle of dark on his thigh. The circle was expanding. I dismissed it as the possibility of us starting to trip. He sponged the spot with his fingers and placed them under the light. His fingers were red.

"Fuck, man," he whined lazily. "You stabbed me."

I hung my head. "Sorry, Matty."

One of the eavesdropping girls screamed.

The hipsters in the kitchen ran out of the house.

"If you were already thinking of bouncing, now might be the time," he said. "These people are snitches and will call the cops for sure."

"Matty, man, I really didn't think I'd get you."

He wiped his fingers on his pant leg. "It's all good."

"Well, you should probably put a Band-Aid or something on that," I laughed.

"You owe me a pair of jeans."

I hopped the fence onto the sidewalk and started a light jog toward home.

. . .

I made the trek incident free, though I was paranoid enough to jump into the bushes every time a vehicle approached. I even convinced myself that if one of those yuppies actually called the cops that I'd have to go back and kill him. Soon as you start mixing chemicals, your brain starts calculating wild conclusions.

What was left of my cocaine amounted to a mole hill on the mirror set horizontal on my desk. I ripped a few lines, lit a cigarette, and lay back on my bed. Free beer. Free K. A little blow. All in all, it was a good night.

In the morning I had four texts from Ed wondering where I disappeared to. The fifth text said that everybody was talking about how I stabbed Matty but they couldn't find either of us. I didn't reply. Like I said, people talk too much.

Upstairs I could hear my mom on the phone talking to her best friend from down the street. I took a shower, got dressed, grabbed my skateboard, and started to head out. It's when my phone rang. I let it ring a couple of times, debating whether I wanted to deal with whoever it was on the other end.

I accepted the call.

"Hey," said a girl's voice.

It was Danielle, my on-again off-again girlfriend. At that point we were on-again, though we might have been off-again. I don't remember. It was hard to keep track.

"Hey."

"You were supposed to call me last night."

"Yeah, I meant too. Ended up at the skate park with Ed and Emily."

"Well I needed to talk to you."

I flung my head back then collapsed my chin to my chest. "Okay," I sighed. "We're talking now."

"I wanted to talk in person."

She makes me want to smash my head against a brick wall.

This time I didn't reply. She broke the silence with, "I'm pregnant."

I still didn't say anything. I could hear her flipping through a magazine. Probably *Cosmo*. It obviously wasn't a big deal to her.

"Aren't you going to say anything?"

"Is it mine?"

"Fuck you, Troy. You're a real asshole, you know that?"

"What do you want me to do?"

"Take me to the clinic."

This is why we were off-again on-again. I can always count on her to do the right thing.

"Today?"

"No. I'm getting my nails done with Emily this afternoon. I called the place we went to last time and they said they have a spot open tomorrow."

"Okay, I can pick you up around lunch."

The line went quiet and I wondered if she hung up. It wouldn't have surprised me. She could be really dramatic at times.

"Um," she said.

"Yeah?"

"Did you stab Matty at a party last night?"

"It's not like that."

"So, you didn't?"

"Not really. Did you want to get together tonight?"

"I don't know. I'll message you."

Another pause. "How do you 'not really–'"

I hung up. It was going to be one of those days.

Matty was always down for a rip, so I headed to his house. His green little four door Honda Civic was parked in the driveway. Being a big guy, Matty always looked funny to see driving such a little car. He didn't care, at least he had a car.

His parents weren't home, so I let myself in.

"Put it away, let's get high," I said, as I opened the door to his room. I was joking. We always said this when one of us showed up unannounced in case the unsuspected was hunched over their bed beating their meat.

His TV was really low but I could hear the moaning cries of two girls going at it. Matty was lying on his couch, back to the girls, one hand reaching behind his naked body shoving what looked like an empty beer bottle up his ass.

My hand snapped to cover my eyes and I jerked my head away. "What the fuck, dude?"

He scrambled off the couch and tossed the prop underneath.

"What the fuck, me? What the fuck, you!" he said. "You can't just barge in here like that."

"What the hell was that?"

He picked up the remote and clicked off the TV. He pulled a blanket over his lower half.

I started to leave.

"What are you doing here?"

"Thought you might want to get high." Looking at him I kept wondering what it was I had just walked in on. The look on his face said he wanted to give me some sort of explanation. So, I said, "What?"

He laughed. "You can't really expect a girl to do it if you wouldn't do it yourself," he said.

I winced. "You're kidding."

"No, I'm a gentleman."

"So, you shove things up your ass, for the ladies?" I gagged.

"You're telling me you've never had a girl put a finger up there?"

"No."

"You should try it sometime."

I shook my head in disgust and rested my hand on the door frame. "Listen, I just came by to see if you wanted to get high, maybe go down to the pier and have a couple brew."

He beamed. "It will change your life."

.   .   .

I waited outside while Matty cleaned up. God knows what else he had up there. I lit a cigarette and gave my pal Robbie a call. No answer. I left a message telling him we were headed down to the pier for a couple pints and he should meet us there.

Matty bounced outside, clicked to unlock his car, "Let's do it."

"How's the leg?"

"Just a little scratch."

"Good."

We stopped by the Beer Store. He ran inside to grab us a couple 40's of Old English. He never got asked for ID on account of his size.

Robbie met us at the pier. His unkempt red goatee, shaved skull, and gothic metal rings weighing his ears made it impossible to miss him in a crowd.

He grinned at me, a feature that always disarmed his biker image, "Is it true you stabbed Matty last night?"

Matty snapped his fingers and shot him the thumbs up. "He sure did, and he's buying me a new pair of jeans."

"It wasn't like that. I don't understand how everybody's already heard. It wasn't that big of a deal."

"Emily's pretty pissed. She said she doesn't want Ed hanging out with you anymore."

"That's bullshit. He'd never choose a chick over me."

"Maybe not, but she's still pretty pissed. You doing that in front of her friends and all."

Matty passed each of us a bottle. We sat in silence watching the waves crash over the pier as people walked their dog's past in the afternoon sun.

Robbie took a swig of his beer. "When are you moving?"

"The landlord said I could move in tomorrow, but I have to take care of some shit in the afternoon, so probably the next day."

"You need a hand?"

"I should be good. I don't have that much stuff to move. Come by after for some drinks though."

We sat drinking our beer for a while. In what seemed like an afterthought, Robbie asked, "What do you have to take care of tomorrow?"

"It's nothing, just some stuff with Danielle."

"You're still going with her?"

"I don't know."

"You didn't get her pregnant again, did you?"

"She says so."

"Dude," Matty interjected. "Why don't you pull out?"

"Or wear a rubber?" Robbie said.

"She's on the pill."

"Well obviously not religious-like if she's pregnant again. You know there's a chance she'll never be able to have kids if she gets another abortion."

"Might be better than all this run around."

"I don't know, man. You're putting a lot on her."

"Are you kidding me? It's a little vacuum they shove up there to suck everything out. It's a twenty-minute procedure that they get you high as fuck for. How is that a big deal? Besides, we're not together. And, I'm taking care of it."

Robbie set his beer on the bench and focused all his attention on me. "Her mom just died, Troy. That's pretty low."

I hate it when people say my name like that. Lecturing me as if I didn't just go through the roller coaster of her mom dying and having to put up with all her self-loathing. Everybody dies. Grieve and get over it.

"Her mom didn't just die. That was three years ago now."

He snatched his beer up, set it to his lips. "You're a real asshole."

"How about instead of riding me for doing the best I can, you ask this guy what he was doing this morning?"

Matty held up his middle finger.

I stood up, threw down my board, and skated away.

The text message read: I need your cock.

It was Jessie. This meant she and her boyfriend had a fight, or he was at work, or he just left. Didn't matter. Meant she was alone and wanted to fuck.

When, where?

Now. My place

OK.

.   .   .

Jessie was a smoke show. Think Christina Aguilera at fifteen. Bleach blonde hair with dark undertones. Petite to the point it made her D cups look even larger. Tanned as if all she ever did was lay by the pool in her bikini. Only she's sixteen. I wish I would've made her when she was fifteen. Fourteen even. But fuck, sixteen was still pretty damn good.

She answered the door, rolled her bottom lip under her teeth, and pulled me inside.

We started making out. Her mouth over mine, our tongues wrestled for dominance. She conceded and started sucking hard on my lip.

In her room she pushed me onto her bed and with a dramatic crawl, mounted my body.

Where she learned the shit, I couldn't be sure. There's no way her boyfriend taught her; he's a pushover piece-of-shit and a rumoured minute man. Probably at one of her shoots.

Jessie is all-natural, and broke into modelling early. Most parents who push their little girl in that direction buy implants and lip enhancements and nose jobs. Not Jessie though, her dad must've been a pervert to know she wouldn't need any adjustments.

Christ, she started doing this motion where she grinds her hips clockwise around my centre and each time she's farthest away she'd squeeze her cunt and not let go until she'd be up at my naval again. This always brought me right near coming, so she'd lift off, release, and then slide down again.

It had to be one of her agents that taught her this. Lift the hips, flip the pelvis, grip the shaft on the way back. Repeat.

I fought to hold on for three passes, but it was no use.

Lying naked and out of breath she told me she wished we didn't have to sneak around like this. She passed me a cigarette.

"We don't."

She lit mine and then one for herself.

We didn't talk the entire time we were smoking. Snubbing out the cigarette she said, "You know I'm with Mitch." With that she got up, pulled on her short-shorts and slipped into a tank top. She left her bra on the floor. She said she had some things to do in the afternoon. My cue to leave.

"Yeah, me too." I crushed my smoke in the ashtray and started to get dressed.

"Talk later?" she said, all innocent like.

"Sure."

At home, my mom had already left for work. My dad was nowhere to be found so I went into their bedroom and opened the top drawer of his giant oak dresser. It was his sock drawer. Buried under all those worn-out socks was an envelope filled with one and five-dollar bills. I took forty dollars' worth and put the envelope back. The envelope was getting pretty thin. I found it the year before and had been lifting from it ever since.

I sat on their bed and opened his nightstand. A bible. A devotional book. A picture of his family when he was a kid and they all lived out west. I'd never met any of his siblings. The picture might as well be from a history textbook, I couldn't even come up with one name.

At the very bottom of the drawer was a framed picture of him and my mom and me when I was only a couple of years old. It's a dark picture but my bright red t-shirt popped against the black background. We looked happy. Maybe that was the last time we were. A car pulled in the driveway. I dropped everything back into the drawer and tiptoed down to my room.

"You can't pull shit like that," Ed said when I answered the phone.

I needed to stop answering my phone. Or get new friends.

"Like what?"

"You're kidding right? You stabbed Matty."

"For God's sake, I didn't stab Matty. Have you talked to him?"

"Yeah, he says you stabbed him."

"Bullshit."

"Yeah, well, he says you owe him a pair of jeans."

"I know. I'm on it."

Ed worked at the Levi's Outlet. We bought all our jeans from him.

"I'll be in tomorrow or something and grab a pair."

"Just wait for me to be on the cash. I'll give you a discount."

"Obviously."

"So, why'd you do it?"

"I was just fooling around and his leg got in the way."

"Jesus."

"What are you saying tonight?" I asked.

"There's that kegger over at the Davidson's."

"Em going?"

"Nah, she has to work. I was going to catch a ride with Robbie. You guys cool? He said you bounced out early from the pier."

"Seriously? What is it with people?"

"He's driving."

We settled on a time and place and hung up.

Goddamn jeans. Goddamn abortion. Goddamn people talking. I pulled a bag of weed from the ceiling, rolled a joint, and smoked it in the backyard.

I spent the rest of the afternoon in my room. I never figured out who pulled in the driveway, and if someone was home, I didn't know they were. Wouldn't surprise me though. My dad was always sneaking around trying to catch me in the "act." Whatever that meant. I just sat there listening to music and playing *The Getaway* on PlayStation. I'd never really been into video games but most of my friends were, so I bought a system and this game to find out what the hype was all about. It was gay. If you're over thirteen and still playing video games, you're gay.

After a bunch of hours staring at the screen, fingers hammering away at the controller, I gave it up and pulled out the *Maxim* from under my mattress to rub one out. The October issue with the Christina Aguilera centrefold. Her on the cover in a white swimsuit, topless. There's a picture of her floating on her back in the ocean. Another of her laying in the sand. The one that does it for me is of her standing by the water, one hand hugging her breasts, the other giving the photographer the finger. Giving me the finger.

It gets me every time.

Mom came home around supper with a bucket of KFC, a box of fries, and some gravy. She said she thought I might be hungry having been out skating all day and asked if I'd eat dinner with her. I hadn't been out skating all day; I left the house with my board and maybe that was my intention, but sometimes days get away from you. Besides, how it turned out with Jessie was just as good a day as hitting some rails. Maybe.

She laid the spread on the table. I sat down across from her.

"Troy," she said. "There's something I want to talk to you about. Your father and I are getting a divorce."

I forced a depressed smile. The type of smile you smile so you don't well up. "I know, Mom."

"I thought you did. I just wanted you to hear it from me."

Her plate hadn't been touched. I doubted she would eat anything. She never did anymore. She had withered to almost nothing, face sullen and sunken around her cheekbones.

"Are you going to be okay, Mom?"

"You know I love you very much," she said. "You're my baby, Troy." She paused, looked down at her plate then looked back up. "Your father, he loves you very much, too."

"What about you though? Where are you going to go? How are you going to live?"

"I'll be fine Troy. I can take a second job."

"You already work full time."

"I'll find a smaller place," she said. "When we sort out all the details, you're going to have to decide who you want to live with. You're old enough to make that decision and I just want you to know that whoever you choose, I love you no matter what."

"I'm moving out, Mom. I found an apartment."

"Oh, Troy," she said. "You don't have to do that. The new place will be big enough for the both of us."

"It'll be good for me. Help me to grow up and all that."

"It seems like only yesterday we moved from that tiny apartment into this place with our very own backyard," she said. "Do you remember crashing through the screen door when you saw the swing set out back?"

I rubbed my chin without realizing it, but then I remembered. "I smashed my chin on the patio or something, didn't I?"

"Your poor little face," she smiled. "You needed three stitches."

I felt for the scar.

"For a month after you wouldn't go in the backyard unless your father carried you through the door."

I don't know why, but suddenly I felt like I wanted to cry. I don't know why but that's how I felt so I stared down at my plate.

She rested her hand on my elbow. "I didn't mean to upset you, honey."

"We were happy once, weren't we?"

She bobbed her head.

"What happened?"

"Life gets complicated."

"That's shit, Mom. Tell me the truth. You had to have been happy to get married."

"You know how I feel about words like that."

She was right. As liberal as she was with everything, she didn't swear and didn't like it when I did. "I'm sorry, Mom," I said. "It just sounds like such a cop out; 'life gets complicated.' People get married because they're in love."

"That's not always true."

"But you two were, right? I've seen the pictures."

"We loved each other, yes."

"And because you were in love, you decided to have a baby?"

She bit her lip, "I know where you're going with this, and you're wrong."

"Then I was born and look where we are now?"

"Troy," she said. "None of this is your fault. You hear me? None of it. This is between me and your father."

"Then what happened?" I flicked a crumb off the table and watched it sail toward the sink.

"Sometimes when things break, they can't be put back together again."

"I don't know why you're giving up so easily."

"We didn't decide this last night," she said. "It's been a long time coming."

"Okay, Mom."

"It's for the best, Troy. We're both miserable."

I shoved a gravy-soaked fry in my mouth. "Sure."

We sat through the rest of the meal in silence. Mom didn't eat anything; every couple of minutes she picked at the fries and dipped them in gravy. She maybe took two bites the entire time.

I stood up. "Do you want me to clean this up?"

"No," she said. "I'll do it. Are you going out tonight?"

I nodded and pushed in my chair.

"Good," she said. "You should be out having fun at your age."

"Mom," I said. "I'm sorry."

"Me too, honey."

"No," I said. "I mean for tonight."

"Why are you sorry?"

"You came home with this treat for dinner, and then I got all upset over nothing."

"It's not nothing."

"No, I shouldn't have got carried away like I did. I love you, mom. I really am sorry."

She pulled me in for a hug and kissed the top of my head.

"It's okay," she said.

A tear escaped the side of my eye and singed my cheek. I palmed it dry and sniffed away what would have been the beginning of a waterfall. "I'll see you later, Mom."

She smiled. "I doubt I'll be awake when you get in."

Robbie picked me up around nine. Ed was sitting in the passenger seat. He smiled and said, "Word on the street is—"

"Yes. I stabbed Matty."

His head wagged. "There you go."

That's all anybody ever wants: to live vicariously through other people's stories. Make it crazy, make it unreal, make it dangerous and everybody wants to talk about it. Fucking convenient how it's almost impossible to verify any of these stories about friends of friends.

"You know Morgan and those girls?" Robbie asked.

"Yeah, Amy and Briar?"

"Amy wants to make you. You're sure that you're finished with Danielle?"

"We're through."

"Good, because I don't think Amy would be down if you had a girlfriend."

"So, what, the three of us for the three of them?"

"I've got Briar, Morgan's for Ed."

"What about Emily?"

"They don't know each other." Ed looked back and winked.

"The lies we lead," I said.

Robbie pulled a three-paper cannon from his glove box and passed it to Ed to light. "I'll smoke to that."

Whenever Robbie smoked and drove, I died. He kept the windows rolled up until we couldn't see each other. Then we'd laugh at how ridiculous the situation was until his tires scraped the curb or he slammed on the brakes inches from rear-ending the car stopped at the stoplight in front of us.

Coughing and stoned, Ed said, "I think that was a cop."

"You're just paranoid."

I opened the window a crack. My half-hearted attempt to clear some of the smoke. Mostly I was just trying to breathe. A car was trailing at a distance; one headlight was dimmer than the other.

"It's not a cop," I said.

"It was a cop."

"Well then open the fucking windows and get some of this smoke out of here," Robbie said.

Smoke poured out of the vehicle. Ed opened the glove box and grabbed the Axe deodorant can. He sprayed it everywhere.

"Dude, you got that in my eyes!" Robbie said.

He slammed on the brakes.

The car behind us flicked on its cherries and any debate about whether it was a cop or not was instantly dismissed. Robbie signalled to turn into the next parking lot. The cruiser followed us in, lights flashing, no siren.

There's no explanation to how we escaped the wrath of the boys in blue. The cop lined us up against the vehicle and patted us down. Besides the joint we'd just smoked, none of us were holding. A surprise to the cop, sure. An even bigger surprise to me. The cop took our names and told Robbie to stop driving around the streets like a hoodlum. Robbie told him we were headed to his place and the cop said that was a good idea and to get going.

Back in the car, Robbie started down the street toward his house. The bastard cop followed. "What a dick," Robbie said, stoned and now hyper vigilant about following all the rules of the road.

Before we'd turned onto Robbie's street, the cop's cherries were back on.

For a moment we all choked. I knew it was too good to be true.

Robbie was about to signal pulling over again when the cop whipped around and sped away in the opposite direction.

Robbie hollered. "Fuck yeah." He pulled the e-brake and fishtailed around like the cop had done. "Time to get to that party."

We made it to the Davidson's. It wasn't hard to miss with a thousand cars parked out front of the house and the roaring fire out back. We pulled up to where a guy sat behind a fold-up poker table. He had a cash box and was taking money from the people coming in. Nobody else was parked there. The guy behind the table glared at Robbie.

"This looks like a good place to park," Robbie said, to no one in particular.

He turned off the car and stepped out.

You can't argue with logic like that.

The guy at the table told us it was five bucks a head. Robbie handed him a twenty.

"Five bucks for parking, too."

Ed flipped him off with a smile.

In exchange for our cash, the guy drew a giant "X" on each of our hands, an "X" that extended far past the wrist. I pulled my hand from his grip. "That's good enough."

"There isn't any beer left anyway, fag," he said. I lurched at him but Robbie clawed me back.

"If I just paid five bucks for this stupid kegger and there's no beer..."

"We'll get our money's worth."

We gravitated toward the kegs. They were still pouring so we grabbed six beers between us, one for each hand. There were people moving in and out of the house. We headed that way next. The kitchen counter was crowded with half empty bottles of liquor. We chugged our beers and filled the cups with vodka and gin.

"Money's worth," Ed said lifting his glass.

"Money's worth," I agreed lifting mine. We cheers'd.

"I'm going to look for the girls," Robbie said.

Ed and I raised our glasses to him.

"Listen, Ed," I said. "I need to make some cash."

"What for?"

"You telling me you couldn't use a couple extra bucks in your pocket?"

"What are you going to do?"

"Reparations for that douche calling me a fag."

Ed followed me upstairs. I went into the first bedroom I found. He stood guard outside.

The Davidson's were spoiled little brats and had every gaming system under the sun. If I could score a PS2 or an Xbox and sneak it back to the car, that'd put at least a couple hundred bucks in my pocket.

I flicked on the light and started poking around the room. I didn't need to. The systems were where they should have been, plugged in under the TV. I figured cash or drugs were better than having to hawk something at the pawnshop so I started nosing around. I shouldn't have turned on the light. It was an amateur mistake. The bedroom window faced out over the fire. I guess someone noticed and asked one of the Davidson's what somebody was doing up in one of their rooms or something to that effect. Before I'd even opened a dresser drawer, I heard a stampede of shoes clamouring up the stairs. Ed kicked his heel against the door and told me to get out. Shy of jumping from the window, I was trapped.

The door burst open. I looked up from my seat on the bed pretending to be surprised. When in doubt choose the boldest way out.

"What the fuck?" I said to the trio who'd arrived with the obvious intention to beat the shit out of whoever was snooping about.

"What the fuck, you!" one of the Davidson's barked. Must have been a school thing because that was always the response any of us gave.

"I'm meeting my girl up here," I lied.

"Get the fuck out of my room," he said. His eyes raged. I swear there was a little puff of steam from his ears.

I stood up and brushed past him. His brother slammed me into the wall. Their friend blocked the doorway.

"This kid wasn't meeting a girl up here," he said to them. "This fag doesn't even like pussy."

I was really getting tired of being called a fag.

"What the fuck were you doing?" the other Davidson barked.

Clever bunch of jocks.

"I told you. I was meeting my girl. Amy texted me like an hour ago, said she'd be up here waiting for me."

"Oh yeah? That's funny. She was never even here."

I looked over at Ed.

He shrugged.

"OK, me too then," I said. "Party's lame." I tried to push past the guy in the doorway but he shoved me. Ed jumped on him with a half nelson and pulled him to the ground.

"Let's go," he yelled.

We shot down the stairs, skipping a half dozen at a time and smashed through the kitchen door to outside. Robbie was standing by his car with a couple of girls. One of us yelled at him to get in and get it started.

Robbie was an excellent driver. He had that thing started and roaring down the driveway before I even closed my door. We hit the main road, he pulled the e-brake and shot stones at some of the people walking home. "Fucking douchebags," he chuckled.

There was a coffee cup filled with soggy cigarette butts in the cup holder. We must have all spotted it at the same time. Ed picked it up and threw it out the window at a guy standing by himself on the side of the road. It hit the kid right in the face.

"Fuck these people," he said.

"Fuck these people," I said, grimacing at the poor sap with cigarette slime dripping from his lips.

In the morning I got up early and asked my mom if I could borrow her car. I told her I was taking Danielle to lunch.

"I really like the two of you together," she said. "I hope you can make it work this time."

That was her giving me permission.

"Thanks, mom."

"Dr. Dimock called; said he'd like to schedule you in for an appointment next week."

"I can't go back there. The guy creeps me out"

"Just give it a chance, Troy. You might be surprised."

"I doubt it."

"You know I see someone, too."

"Is that supposed to make me feel better?"

"It takes a pretty strong person to ask for help," she said. "Just so you know."

"Don't give me that, Mom. I'll go if I have to, just don't feed me crap."

"It's not crap."

"I'll bring your car back by dinner."

Her face fell. At least it wasn't a blank stare.

"Hey, Mom," I said. I knew I shouldn't. "Do you think I could borrow some money?"

She almost smiled. "How much do you need?"

Danielle's eyes were swollen. She looked like she hadn't slept. It could have been that she'd been up all night with one of her girlfriends. No doubt she'd start bragging that the two of them polished off twenty-four beers to themselves. That or how they ate a bag of mushrooms and tripped out playing Ouija all night.

These are the types of things she said she does with her girlfriends. Girlfriends who in four years I have somehow never met. Of course I didn't believe her. Danielle is tiny. It's practically physically impossible to drink like that. Still, she told me these things. Maybe it was her way of coping with the death of her mom.

When her mom was in the hospital, she'd boast about how her dad didn't dare discipline her because of her mom's brain tumour. He wrote it off for that exact reason. Her mom was dying of cancer, it was okay to act out in order to cope with the stress. At the time I thought she was trying to impress me, flaunting her independence, even though I'd never done drugs before and hadn't yet learned it wasn't only the cool kids who did them.

What I wanted to say when she was going through it all was that if she needed a hug, I was always there for her. I would have held her for days. I hated seeing her all fucked up the way she was. But I didn't know how to talk to her. I didn't know what to do. So, I did nothing.

I knew I couldn't blame her. She was about to lose her mom and her dad was a dick. As soon as her mother slipped into a coma her dad openly started seeing a new woman.

I remember after the funeral, she pulled out a little joint and passed it to me to light. That was my first taste of weed. Really though, I'm not putting this on her.

．　　．　　．

"Just drive," she said.

Just drive. The words were so thick I could tongue them. One day you're head over heels in love. The next, just drive.

I drove the Queen Elizabeth Highway past the 406, then out and out. I watched a hundred wineries pass in the rear-view mirror. Wineries Danielle and I had once toured with her older sister and her sister's boyfriend.

All of those days behind us.

We were sixteen the first time she got pregnant. Those stories about people who have sex once and get pregnant, the ones about kids not trying to and getting pregnant when there are a million happily in-love couples trying who can't. That was us.

Young. Dumb. Full of cum. Pregnant.

My mom had a van back then and every once in a while, I was allowed to borrow it if Danielle and I were going on a date. This time, I picked her up to go and see the new *Mission Impossible*.

I'd been trying to lay her for months. All my friends were bragging about balling girls and I practically begged her to. We were virgins.

If she loved me, she would, I'd say.

I would always be there, I'd lie.

That night, three years ago now, when I picked her up, she was tense. I asked her what was wrong. "Nothing." I signalled to get on the highway and head to the theatre when she told me to keep driving. "Where?" I said.

"Just drive."

We drove down the service road parallel the highway. When we approached the park by the lake, she said to turn in.

I did. I thought I knew what she was doing, I felt a pressure building in my jeans.

I parked my mother's van in the parking lot. We sat there, staring out over the lake for what felt like hours but was probably only the length of "Otherside" by The Chili Peppers.

She turned to me and said, "I'm ready."

She handed me a condom, unfastened her seat belt and climbed over the seat.

I bumbled out the door and hurried around to her side.

She pulled me close and we started kissing. It was that moment in a dream when you know what's going to happen but can't wake up. Stuck. I struggled. She pulled her jeans down. We got the condom on and before she pained her second moan, I finished.

I remember thinking, is that all it is?

The look in her eyes begged the same question.

As the story goes, the condom broke. But I didn't know. I just threw it out the window and thought the mess was normal. A few weeks later she missed her period. I told her I was hers. I told her I meant everything I said. This entire time I was praying to a God I didn't believe in, pleading with him to make her suggest an abortion.

It's the only time I thought God answered prayers.

. . .

When I was a kid, whenever we travelled as a family, my mom, my dad and me, we'd listen to stories on cassette. My parents thought it was better than all the secular messages on the radio. They were pretty religious back then. We had three series we'd rotate through: *Adventures in Odyssey*, *Sherlock Holmes*, and *The Lone Ranger*.

My mom must have hated driving in silence. Maybe she was afraid of being alone. All I know is that as Danielle and I drove the highway to the clinic this second time, some British bloke narrated Doyle's *A Study in Scarlet*.

We didn't say a word. Stories on tape work like magic.

We pulled into the clinic's parking lot. I rolled down the window and pressed the blue lighted button on the parking gate to release a ticket.

"Do you love me?" Danielle asked, staring straight ahead.

The gate lifted and I drove the car in the direction of her gaze.

I pulled into the first vacant space and parked.

Danielle looked at me. She wanted an answer.

"Why are you asking me that?"

"I want to know."

"Are you having second thoughts about the baby?"

"Don't call it that."

God, I could use some blow, I thought. "Well are you having second thoughts?"

"I want to know if you love me."

"I want to know why you want to know."

"You're a real asshole."

"Yeah, you've said that before." I said. "Do you want me to come in with you?"

"I'm not going in there by myself and sitting with all those kids getting abortions beside each of their parents sitting there in condescension."

"Then I'll come in and support you."

"I don't want your support."

I stared at the steering wheel. You want me to sit in condescension? I knew better than to say anything like that out loud.

"I want everyone to look at you like I do. Troy the Asshole, Troy the Bitch, making me get another abortion."

"I'm not making you do anything."

"Then answer the question."

I didn't want to look at her so I didn't. I just kept staring at the steering wheel.

"Get the procedure."

"Really, procedure? It's a fucking abortion and it's you murdering our child. Again."

"I never told you to do this."

"You just did."

She slammed the door. I slammed my hand on the steering wheel and screamed; nothing even coherent, just a frustrated scream. She stood in the parking lot, hand on her hip, smirking, staring at me with the attitude of "are you coming?"

. . .

The waiting room was packed, same as the parking lot. A dozen young girls and a dozen parents glared at me as we walked in. It didn't matter, my mind was elsewhere. All I could think of was that this clinic had their business on lock down. There were two vacant seats near the only other door in the room and I assumed that's where the girls went into get prepped.

Danielle checked-in with the receptionist. We sat down in the empty seats. All the parents accompanying their promiscuous children stared me down like I had knocked up their own baby girls. Some of the girls looked at me like they wished I'd had.

It was an assembly line. More girls were called in as others exited that solitary door beside us. Tears lined the eyes of most of the girls still waiting their turn. I picked up a magazine but couldn't read. Aside from contemplating a way to get one of these girls' phone numbers, I was thinking about the tape in the car and the trial Holmes was about to sit through and if by Thursday he'll have had enough time to solve the mystery. Sherlock Holmes always solved the mystery, so really, I was thinking about nothing.

An hour later, Danielle came out of the door wearing the same blank face as all the other girls who had preceded her. She walked through the room mechanically and stopped at the reception window. The lady handed her a manila envelope. The papers inside would tell her what to expect over the next few weeks, who to call if there were any complications, and most importantly what she could and couldn't do. Namely, no sex for six weeks. I still remembered that from the first time. Package in hand, Danielle left the office. I followed, face turned down, acutely aware of all the eyes burning cigarette holes in my back. No doubt all these parents would be talking about me to their best friends who lived down their own streets later that evening.

"Do you ever think about what it was like before all of this?"

This is the first thing Danielle said to me after we left the clinic. I could only guess what she was referring to. Before the abortions? Before her mom? I'd be more interested in what prompted the question. Maybe her drugs were wearing off.

The familiar smell of the lake blew over the highway. The burned down and abandoned ship moored to the entrance of the harbour appeared ahead. The harbour beside the park where we first had sex. The park where she first got pregnant. Where we first got pregnant. The ship that burned the same year her mother died. Arson, allegedly.

I'd love to get my hands on those little punks who thought it was funny to set the relic ablaze. Not that I wouldn't have done the same if I'd considered it first, but Danielle and her mom used to go there every Sunday for lunch. Sometimes they'd stay for hours. After they ate, they sat on the rocks and stared at the woodwork casing the ship. They were close. They talked, they laughed; it was Danielle's favourite day. They loved that ship, now it's a floating hunk of rusted steel, two naked masts erect against the clouded sky. This abandoned ship was the salt to her wound.

Have I ever thought about what it was like before all of this? At least it's better than, "just drive."

"No," I said, finally. "I don't. I haven't. As much as I tend to think about everything, I don't like thinking backward."

Danielle pursed her lips. Her eyes followed the ship. I signalled to exit the highway and drove slowly off the ramp.

She spoke hesitantly, "Will you come with me to the cemetery?"

Robbie was right. Danielle was right. I am an asshole.

Only not today.

"Of course," I said, and rested my hand on her knee.

I didn't know if it was still there, but at one time there was a garden nursery near the cemetery. Sunrise Nursery. When I turned onto Fourth Street, I saw the large storefront and adjacent glass building. The illuminated sign read "Open."

"Should we get some flowers?" I asked.

Danielle didn't say anything. I don't think she could have spoken if she wanted to, but she nodded.

We stopped at the nursery to pick up some flowers and left with two white English rose bushes instead. One thing we both agreed on is there's nothing more depressing than dead flowers on a grave. It's important to find common ground in relationships; at least that's what I've heard.

The cemetery where her mom is buried is at the top of a tree-lined hill behind a tiny cobblestone church built sometime in the late 1800's. For being so old, there aren't very many graves. Which is surprising because most cemeteries keep growing and growing until they come up against property owners who won't sell. I think for this place you had to be related to one of the church's founding member's family. Something divisive like that. Leave it to the church to be divisive.

It's impossible to escape the selfishness of human nature. Even now, in her moment of anguish, both for her mom and this fresh loss, on some level I'm hoping I'll get laid, or at least be on the receiving end of a blowjob.
There wasn't anybody at the cemetery when we arrived.

We sat silently in the car. Danielle stared at the floor. She squirmed in her seat. I placed my hand on her thigh and gave her a little squeeze. I wanted to apologize for being such a dick these past couple of days; these past few years. I wanted to hold her and let her cry. To cry with her like I should have all those years before. To lose your mom as a teenage girl, to be left with a fucked-up dad and a shitty boyfriend; I couldn't even imagine. Guilt is easy to ignore when it's not staring you straight in the face.

She cleared her throat, paused, and said, "I'm ready."

I found a blanket in the trunk. We unrolled it in front of her mother's headstone. Danielle leaned heavily into the crux of my shoulder as I held tight around hers. Her hair smelled the same as the first time I met her. It's funny what a scent can do, how it can bring you back to somewhere long forgotten.

Growing up, my parents belonged to an evangelical missionary church. Nominal participation wasn't an option. I think Jesus said somewhere that he hated lukewarm followers and my parents made certain we would never be even remotely tepid. That meant aside from Sunday mornings, they had Monday night study groups. Which meant we had Wednesday evening worship service, and I had Friday night youth group. A forced type of fun.

Friday night youth group always started with a short welcome from the group leader, followed by a couple secular sounding rock praise songs like "Jesus Freak" and "Delirious" and hymns redubbed with heavy drums and the occasional guitar riff. They wanted to attract the youth who hadn't yet been indoctrinated into the church. Capture and assimilate. It was shit for us though, the already indoctrinated. We were second-rate compared to the outsiders, like banks who offer free TV's for opening a new account with them, not valid for existing customers. Come to our free, fun event, in exchange for sitting through some babble about immaculate conception and magic and resurrection; but if you're already one of us, sit in the back and shut your mouth.

We'd break off into groups, usually by sex, and begin whatever activity was planned. At the end of the evening, the canteen would open and sell discounted snacks, and we'd get the opportunity to flirt with our crushes from the other group while waiting for our parents.

This is where I met Danielle, but before Danielle, Friday night youth group is where I met my best friend, Casey. His family was part of the church first. We'd only just moved to town and when my parents started attending the Word of Life community, Casey and I became friends by proximity. What I mean is under normal circumstances he and I wouldn't have necessarily gravitated toward each other. It wasn't like I would have picked him first for baseball or street hockey. He was small, awkward, and wore really dumb glasses. Not quite coke bottles, but thick frames, and squared; something like the modern hipster look. His clothes were always clean and obviously laid out for him by his mother. In any other situation we would have never talked.

On these forced fun nights though, the pickings were slim. His nerd facade was transformed into a kind of "cool by comparison" and we started to get to know each other. Casey was fucking fearless. If a ball got stuck in the rafters during an indoor soccer game, he'd scurry up the basketball net, swing over to the caged clock on the wall and pull himself to a standing position on top of the wire. Then he'd monkey bar across the rafters toward the lodged ball, chuck it down, and reverse the process all the way back. The ceiling had to be at least three stories high. No joke.

It wasn't long after these first encounters that became inseparable. Even though we lived across town from each other we'd spend every moment we could together. Weekend adventures at the Old Mill. Deconstructing everything we could get our hands on and then building something new from the pieces. Obviously, there was paintball and fireworks and exploring abandoned buildings. That kind of inseparable.

He's how I met Danielle. His parents had non-religious friends, so for the most part she didn't come to the church stuff. Fridays were peddled as more of a fun time than religious though, despite the completely blatant message, so Danielle started coming out on Friday nights.

I fell for her the second she flashed her harmony brown eyes at me. Those little freckles that dotted her cheeks and disappeared when she smiled. Her thick straight hair that barely brushed her shoulders. She was a dream. She still is.

"Where are you?" Danielle said, oblivious to me being lost in a memory long since passed.

"I was just thinking," I said.

"About?"

"You. When we first met."

Danielle settled back into my shoulder and started tracing her fingers on my chest.

"When was the last time you visited Casey?"

"I don't."

We sat embraced until the sun, once burning white in the sky, became yellow and had turned orange in its descent. Danielle was picking at the plastic around the pot of the rose bushes so I suggested we dug them in before it got dark. The thing was, we didn't have a shovel.

There was a little shed behind the church. I presumed it was home to the lawnmower and hoses and garden tools. They had to keep the stuff somewhere and it just made sense that this little shed was the place.

It was locked.

I thought about kicking the door in, just one little kick near the handle would have jumped the latch, but being Danielle's mom's final resting place and all, I decided against it.

"Well," I said. "Do you know where you want them planted?"

"You didn't find a shovel," she said.

I shrugged. "Doesn't matter. Where were you thinking?"

She looked at the headstone.

In front of the marble was a lightly manicured patch of dirt with a rock border encasing perennials of gay feather and hummingbird mint. Most likely because they didn't need any tending and always returned year after year.

"I was thinking if we planted one on each side they could climb up and get tangled together on top. I think the roses would look pretty encasing the stone."

I didn't know if these rose bushes climbed like vines, but I wasn't going to argue. There's that saying: You can be right or you can be happy.

Kneeling in front of Danielle's mother's headstone, I pulled a rock from the border and began digging with it. I didn't look up at Danielle. I just dug like I *just drove*, except just digging didn't hold any tainted memories. Just digging was what needed to be done, so just digging was the right thing to do.

The first bush was planted and as I was moving to dig the second one in, I caught a glimpse of Danielle's face. Tears streamed from the corner of her eyes. She was trying to still her trembling lips with no success.

"Oh, sweetheart," I started to say.

She threw her arms around me. "I love you, Troy."

It was only the drugs wearing off, and the flood of memories, and the stress of the day, but I stopped working and held her. We hugged. "I love you, too," I whispered. Partly because I did love her, but mostly because saying I love you is a social contract that will break down if one person says it and the other doesn't.

My hands were dirty. I had mud under my fingernails. It hurt to think how we got here.

"I wish we could go back," she said.

"Me too," I said silently.

Danielle kissed me. I kissed her. Somehow, we were back at the car. Those moments from seated to now were lost in translation.

Her mom isn't buried far from her house. Before I even realized I'd driven Danielle home, she was shutting the door behind her. She walked around to my side of the car, rested her hand on my arm and said thank you.

I made the face you force for empathy: lips tucked in; cheeks slightly puffed out; a shallow nod. The same kind of face I gave my mom when I faked a smile. The same face Danielle gave me earlier.

All of us faking something.

"Got any blow?" I shouldn't have called Robbie.

"Yeah man, what do you need?"

"Like a gram. Maybe a half." I paused. It always turns out more than you planned on. "How much for a ball?"

"You going on a rip?" he replied.

"I don't know, what are you up to?"

"Was thinking about heading down to Murphy's for a couple pints."

"Yeah, that works. I'll meet you there."

During the summers, Casey and I hung out pretty much every day. Soon as school kicked in, we'd only get to hang out on Saturdays. I lived in town and Casey on the outskirts, so he was bused to school. Each Saturday we'd hop on our bikes and meet half-way.

Half-way was the Old Mill; one of those crumbling stone buildings with a rotted-out water wheel that hung above a receded water line. At one time it would have been a landmark, pivotal to the development of the area, but now it was tucked away and forgotten like a senior emaciating in a long-term care facility.

We saw it as another casualty of all-consuming progress and liked to imagine ourselves born in a time before then.

The Old Mill was the cornerstone for all our adventures. Even though we'd explored it a thousand times, sifting through the old rubble in search of buried treasures was a task that could never be exhausted. We'd pull out all sorts of things from that mess: old prohibition bottles speckled in moss, first-aid kits with soiled bandages in rolls, rusted tackle boxes filled with wooden hand-painted lures, and on rare finds, bone carved pocket knives. My favourite was when we found folded yellowed newspapers from nineteen thirty something. One of them had an article on the front page that explained how to use borax as an eye wash for weak or inflamed eyes. The article also said that it could be used as an oral rinse to be swallowed to relieve hoarseness. We'd laugh thinking about how many people this advice knocked off the living list.

Behind the Old Mill and down the ravine was government land, with a river passing through the middle of it.

The Old Mill was our playground. We'd hike, swim, fish; we'd spend the whole day exploring. We'd play a type of hide-and-seek where one of us would run off and the other would have to stalk the runner without being caught and then report back what the evader had been doing all morning. It made us incredibly stealthy. We'd set traps that only we knew about and if anybody ever chased us through the woods, we could lead them over and get away cleanly.

Nobody had ever chased us, but it was empowering to know that we'd have the upper hand.

We knew the woods so thoroughly we could navigate them in the dark. Every dip in the ground, every unexpected drop, every downed tree, every rock, every bend in the river and its depth as it flowed from the Old Mill to wherever it flowed in to.

The Old Mill was our sanctuary. Nobody ever bothered us there. It was ours, and we could do whatever we wanted.

At school we were studying the FLQ crisis in Quebec. Don't ask me what FLQ stands for, it doesn't matter anyway. In that class we learned how the FLQ used homemade bombs to inflict their mayhem. I never understood why they taught us these details in class or why other students didn't find these anecdotes as alluring as we had, but when the teacher spoke the word "homemade," I shot a glance at Casey. As soon as class was dismissed, we went to the library and searched the internet for instructions.

Between the two of us, we had everything we needed to make our own. The Jolly Roger Cookbook told us so.

I had a pellet rifle and firecrackers, M80's, so it was my responsibility to bring those. M-80's are big-ass firecrackers and would serve nicely as a fuse. Casey's job was to bring a canning jar of gasoline and as much Styrofoam he could get his hands on. Our version wouldn't exactly be like the Molotov and fertilizer ones the FLQ used, but we expected a similar effect. The firecrackers were an addition so we could rig up the jar to detonate when we shot at it with the pellet gun. Usually we operated under the "Safety Third" rule but having never set one of these off we figured being a far distance away from the explosion was a good idea. Still, more important than safety was the fact that something blowing up because you shot it, was awesome.

When I arrived at the Old Mill, Casey's bike was already there. I laid mine against his and walked to the edge of the escarpment to see if I could spot him. He was sitting on a flat rock with his feet in the water.

"Hey Case," I called down.

He turned and waved. "Hey, man."

Even from where I stood, I could see them. No matter what, they always made me wince.

"What the fuck, Case?"

"It looks worse than it is," he said.

I climbed down the ravine to where he sat.

Close-up it was worse.

The bruises went from black to blue around his eye and brown to yellow at the edges. Where it should have been the white of his eye was completely red. His lips were swollen to twice their size and the skin above his nose was cut in three places.

"You've got to get out of there, Case," I said. "We would put you up no problem."

I put my hand on his shoulder and he started to cry.

"I thought the last time would be the last time." His breath shuddered between sobs. "I always think it's the last time."

"Fuck him, Case. You don't deserve this. He doesn't deserve you. Let's just get you out of there."

He squared his shoulder away from my touch and chucked a rock into the river. "Fuck!"

Casey rarely swore. I handed him another rock and Casey chucked that one too. We stood in silence for what felt like thirty minutes. It was probably only three. I didn't know what to say, so I changed the subject. "I guess you didn't bring the gasoline, did you?"

He wiped the tears with his sleeve, shook his head no, then smiled. "Of course, I did. Packed it as soon as I got home from school."

"Let's rig it up then."

"I was thinking we should do it on the landing."

Down the river was a flat rock we dubbed 'the landing.' It was our rendezvous point if we ever got separated while exploring. Our contingency plan was as soon as either of us noticed we were alone we were to search for the other for ten minutes and if we didn't make contact, we were to head the rock and wait for the other to show up.

The landing also happened to be the best place to blow shit up.

As we walked toward the rock, we picked up stones and threw them in the river.

"Remember that time we tried to dam the water?" Casey asked.

"We lugged those rocks all day."

"We weren't even close," he laughed. "What a good time though."

We rigged everything up on the rock and doubled back behind some boulders where we'd have shelter from the exploding glass and whatever else might get kicked up in the process.

I passed Casey the gun. "You shoot it."

"Yeah?" he asked.

"Of course." It was the least I could do.

"Thanks, man."

Casey was one hell of a shot; even with the injuries to his face. No sooner could you hear the click of the trigger on the rifle did we both fall back laughing from the heat of the flaming mushroom. I don't know who said it first, but we both agreed, "That was awesome."

Murphy's was dead. The dart boards weren't being used. The tables were empty. The only person seated at the bar was Bart. He sat where he always sat, at the end, in front of the video machine. He was playing Solitaire or whatever he played each time I stumbled into this place.

I got the nod from him and sat down a few seats away.

The bartender, Steph, gave me the eye like I never called her after the other night. I hadn't, so I shrugged an apology.

"Budweiser," Steph said, not waiting for my answer.

Steph was smaller than me. Built like those girls in female muscle magazines. Five-foot-four and great tits. Her hair was always in a ponytail and she talked with a sharp octave that if sped up would be annoying, but with her cadence makes you want to lay her to hear the way she'll talk to you in bed and scream when she's orgasming.

A couple weeks back she took me home. Her and her sister. It wasn't exactly like that, though her sister was just as involved as anybody I'd ever experienced. They're a great team. Obviously, I wish it would have been her and her sister for the final act, but only spoiled brats get everything they want.

We were drinking. I assumed it was her house, Steph's. Then their dad came home. They heard his car pull in the driveway and told me to get behind the couch. I left my beer on this oak carved coaster on the table and crouched down behind the couch. We were blitzed from doing rails all night and the only reason we were drinking beer was to level out. I'd just opened the beer and as I was crouching, I hoped it would still be cold when I could stand up again.

Their dad came in the house like a drunk bull. Steph and her sister began grovelling at this pathetic excuse of a man. They were laughing at his less than rape-like innuendos. I wanted to jump out from behind the couch and beat the shit out of him. How a father with two girls as nice as Steph and her sister could be such an asshole blows my mind. I peeked around the couch and caught eyes with Steph. They told me to wait.

"I know you have some punk here," he said.

"No daddy, we were waiting for you," they said in unison, eerily *Shining*-like.

"I ain't no chump, I can see his beer right there."

I knew I should have grabbed my beer.

"No daddy," her sister said. "We opened that for you."

Silence.

"I'll take it in my room." I heard him leave.

I heard one of the girls pick up my beer and follow him down the hall. I heard a door shut.

I stayed crouched behind the couch for some time. I felt a tap on my shoulder. It was Steph. She held one finger to her lips and motioned for me to follow. I did. She handed me her sister's beer and led me to a bedroom. Her bedroom, I think.

I tried to ask her what that was all about but she wouldn't let me speak.

With one finger on her lips, she used her other hand to slip off her pants.

She undid my belt. Slid off my pants. Started kissing me and whispered, "Don't you dare make a fucking sound."

In the other room, I could hear the grunts of her father. I could hear fake pleasure moans from her sister. Before I could rationalize any of it, I was hard. I didn't know if it was the thought of her dad fucking her sister, or that after all this time I'd finally closed the deal with Steph. That's a lie, I knew it was the former. I started imagining that the stubble on my face brushing Steph's cheek, was her father's hairs rubbing against her sister's face.

It was the best orgasm I'd ever had.

Steph had her back to me while she loaded clean glasses in the fridge below the liquor counter. Robbie walked in wearing a trench coat. He shook hands with Bart, out of respect, then cocked his head signalling me to meet him out back. Steph rolled her eyes, she didn't like Robbie.

I followed him down the hall and out the back door.

"I need your help with something."

"What's up?"

"Last week this guy ripped me off. Shitty coke."

"What do you need me for?"

"I'm getting him to meet us here," he said. "I want you to sit in and try the blow."

"Is it rat poison or something?"

"No, no, it's usually good. He just gets stupid every once in a while and cuts it too much. Baby laxative, baking soda, that sort of thing. He isn't dumb enough to do it twice in a row, so it's really just a free line. You my man?"

"I got you."

A red Nissan pulled behind the bar. Robbie and I climbed into the back seat. The guy had his girlfriend with him, she was driving. She was pregnant or had the biggest gut I'd ever seen.

Buddy pointed at me. "Who's this?"

"Quality control."

"About last time, it wasn't from my usual guy. I didn't know."

"Whatever, I have to take precautions now. Cut him a line."

He cut me a line. His girlfriend turned off the ignition.

She was black. Not that it matters. The pregnant junkie bitch.

I sniffed the line. The coke started to drip down the back of my throat. Half my face numbed. It was good. I widened my eyes like the start of a roll and quick sniffed for good measure.

"What do you think?" Robbie asked.

I grinned. "It's good."

"Only last time it wasn't," Robbie teethed.

"I told you it wasn't my usual stuff. I didn't mean anything by it. Honest."

Robbie pulled a gun from his coat and pressed it against the side of buddy's head. The girlfriend screamed. I slid against the door. I'm pretty sure my jaw dropped.

"Shut up, bitch," Robbie said to the girl, gun glued to her boyfriend's temple.

"What the fuck, man?" buddy said. He raised his hands slightly, but otherwise maintained his composure. "Your friend said it was good."

Robbie chuckled. "Yeah, but this is for last time."

"Put the gun down. You can take what I have. We'll call it even."

Buddy reached toward the glove box. I assumed he was reaching for the rest of the cocaine. His junkie girlfriend must have thought the same thing because she latched onto Robbie's arm like a little girl on her daddy's leg when she doesn't want him to leave. The guy grabbed at the gun and both started pulling. Robbie ended up yanked over the front seat, face planted at buddy's feet. He never let go of the gun. Buddy started punching at him like a cornered cage fighter, just smashing what he could of Robbie with his forearm. Robbie was kicking wildly. The girl kept screaming. Everything happened so fast and with that line I snorted just seconds before I hadn't moved from my position against the door.

Robbie yelled at me, "Get out of the car! Get this fucking guy off me!"

I totally should have thought of that. The coke was really quite good.

I got out, opened the passenger door and tried to lock the guy in a Nelson. It worked for Ed at the party, I thought it could work for me. I saw the bag of blow on the floor and made move for it. Buddy broke free of my grip. Then I noticed a bat beside the seat and him reaching toward it. Robbie dropped the gun. I grabbed the bat and swung it at the guy's face. His nose erupted a mist of red. He was wearing these dumb swollen hoop earrings and I suddenly had the urge to yank them out. I was raging. He let go of Robbie.

Robbie scrambled over top of him. He scooped up the gun on the way out the door. Buddy gripped his bloodied face. The girlfriend hugged her stomach. Instead of screaming, now she cried, wailed even. Buddy was yelling something. Robbie pulled the slide of the gun and released it. The abrupt stop of metal on metal when the slide locked itself in place charged the air. It's the unmistakable sound for a loaded gun. It's upping the ante. He stood over buddy and pressed it to his head. The yelling stopped. The girlfriend's crying became sobs.

Bat in my hand I swung again. It's powerful to swing a bat. This time I aimed at buddy's window. The glass exploded in his face. Robbie must have saw me wind up because he didn't even flinch. He kept the gun trained. I smashed the back-passenger window and started circling the car smashing all the glass as I made my way around.

Robbie was saying something to the guy, but I couldn't hear shit. I was on a rampage. Adrenaline surged. I reached the driver's side. The girl sat stunned, staring at me from behind the glass. I wound up. She raised her hands in defence. A useless gesture. Hands up don't shoot. I hesitated. Her hands were covered in blood. Why were her hands covered in blood?

Her lap was soaked in a viscous red.

I froze. Guys should never bring their girls to business deals.

The freezing lasted only a second. I decided to swing. Fuck her. Just as I'm about to come down with the bat, Robbie pulled at me.

We started running.

The only thing I had on my mind was: Steph is going to be pissed.

Robbie's friend Bart was waiting for us down the street. He said he saw the whole thing. Said it was wild. We got in his car and sped off.

"Where's your wheels?" I asked Robbie.

"I parked by the Beer Store."

Bart slapped Robbie's knee. "You guys are a riot. That was fucking awesome."

He dropped us off and said we should probably stay away from Murphy's for a while.

Robbie's phone rang. It was buddy. Robbie answered anyway.

"You're a dead man," I heard him scream.

Robbie told him to fuck off and hung up.

In the distance we could hear sirens. Probably for us.

It was time to disappear.

I gave it to Robbie when we got in his car.

"What the fuck was that, man? Murphy's is where I drink."

I realized I was still holding the bat.

He grinned. "Not anymore."

"Where are we going now?"

"Strippers. I need a drink."

"I could use a line."

"I don't have any."

"I do," I smiled. "I scooped his."

"My man!"

I wiped the bat on my hoodie, careful not to rip it on the shards of glass embedded in the wood, but firm enough to clean my prints off, and tossed the bat out the window. I pulled the bag of coke from my pocket. There had to be at least an eight-ball in it. I cut half a dozen lines on the back of a CD. Every red light, I passed it to him to huff and then took one for myself. We called it the red-light game.

Robbie left his trench coat in the car. Where he got a trench coat from, I don't know. I was glad he took it off though. He looked like one of those Columbine kids. Then I remembered the piece he pulled.

"Where'd you get a gun from?"

He laughed. "It's a BB gun. Walmart special."

We knew a couple of the strippers at the club. When we sat down, they came over.

"I thought you were taking me shopping, Troy," Alexis said.

Alexis started stripping a year ago. She looked like Jessie, only older. Alexis said she was stripping to pay her way through college. Her real name was Janet. My bet is she'll be stripping long past when she is supposed to graduate from college.

Last time I came by the club I told her I would take her shopping in the States. I got wasted and slept through her call.

"Lexi, baby," I said. "My phone died."

She scanned the club. The tables were filled with tired old men in drab sweaters. I could see her debating if she wanted to earn some money or do some blow. She tapped her finger against her lip in metronomic rhythm. When put against the other, drugs will always prevail.

"Cut me a line?" she finally asked.

After four or five pitchers we decided to call it a night. That, and we ran out of blow. Well, I told Robbie we ran out of blow. I figured he owed me for the stunt he pulled, and besides, I was the one who nabbed it.

We said goodbye to Alexis and the other girls and sped off toward the highway. KMFDM's new song, "WWIII," started to play on the radio. I turned it up. It's an epic song. It starts off real slow, all blue grassy, then drops into hard core metal. I told Robbie to listen. He started bobbing his head to the blues. I noticed our exit approaching, but the drums were about to kick in and I didn't want to steal the experience from him, so I didn't say anything. It really is that good of a song. Just as the drums exploded, Robbie realized what I foresaw and made his move. Too late.

We swerved across two lanes of highway and struck the median. We bounced in our seats. The car uprooted the first sign. Its posts snapped like twigs and the metal sheet smashed the windshield. Before we could wipe the glass from our faces, we hit the second sign. Bigger. It crashed down on the roof of the car. As Robbie made the final merge over the second curb and onto the ramp, we struck the third sign. Instantly airborne, it crashed down and sliced through the roof behind his head. I've said it before: Robbie is a master behind the wheel. I'm sure if it was anybody else in the driver's seat, we wouldn't have survived.

We followed the ramp around the bend. I remember thinking we looked just like one of those Mothers Against Drunk Driving commercials they had on TV that I always thought looked fake. I almost started laughing. Robbie looked at me, wide-eyed. "Keep going?"

"Definitely keep going."

Driving at 120, no windshield, we nearly froze to death ripping down that stretch of road. I thought I glimpsed a car following us, and said so.

Robbie dismissed me. "You're just paranoid. We're only a few blocks from home. We'll make it. Then we'll tarp the car and deal with it in the morning."

Famous last words. Or is it famous first words? We turned onto the final stretch of road and found ourselves boxed in by four cruisers. Lights flashing, sirens blaring. The lead cruiser slammed on his brakes. Robbie was forced to do the same. The cruiser tailing us followed suit, right up his ass. Another cruiser flew up on the left, squealed to a last-minute stop. The fourth jumped the curb to our right, and skidded his aggression on the grass. They were very dramatic. We were very fucked. Well, at least Robbie would be. If they didn't find the blow on me, I'd probably be fine.

Wide-eyed like before, Robbie stared at me. "I'm going to lie."

"Definitely lie."

Other cars crawled by. I finally realized what people meant when they said rubbernecking. It really did look like people had rubber necks.

Robbie rolled down his window. A hovering giant skinhead cop stood outside.

"You boys been in an accident?" he asked. Not only were these policemen dramatic, they were observant. At least they weren't chicks. Female cops are insufferable. They have a hard-on for balls.

"No, officer," Robbie said.

My eyebrows scrunched as I tried to hide my smirk.

Robbie proceeded to tell him what happened.

"We were at the strippers having a couple drinks after work, you know?"

When you lie, it's best to use specifics.

"When we were leaving, there was a black man getting into my car and he took off with it. The guy stole my car!"

Jesus wept.

"We found it like this and figured I'd just drive it home," he said.

The cop struggled to restrain his own smile.

I stared straight ahead. I was sure I looked like Robbie had when he first hit the signs.

This was either a bold move or completely dumb.

The cop retreated to his cruiser.

"Quick on my feet, huh?"

I shone him a hesitant smile.

The giant skinhead cop reappeared in the window. There was a knock on mine.

I wrenched the handle to roll it down.

I had to duck a little to see the officer's face. His barrel chest filled the entire frame.

He was the biggest cop I'd ever seen. Linebacker big. Angry looking like one of those black guys who grew up in the Panthers and was pissed he had to integrate with Whitey.

I looked at Robbie. He looked at me. Now we were both making that stupid wide-eyed face.

"Tell me the truth and I'll let you off easy," the skinhead said.

Robbie paused. One thing is certain, you can never trust cops. You can never trust anyone for that matter. I sat there while Robbie contemplated the offer. I wondered if he'd repeat his initial statement or if he'd try something else.

Like a machine gun firing, Robbie exploded, "We were at the strip club had a couple pitchers missed the on ramp hit a sign decided to keep driving." Inhale.

The skinhead cop smiled. The black cop smiled.

"You're going to have to step out of your vehicle."

Robbie was seated in the back of the cop car. I was seated beside my guard. The coke in my pocket was burning a hole. I opted for a cigarette instead.

"Can I get out and have a smoke?"

"If you run, I'll beat you down."

I believed him. "I won't run."

"I'm watching you." He raised his right hand, flashed two fingers, pointed them at his eyes before very slowly turning them toward me. He cocked his hand into a gun and pulled the trigger. He winked before blowing the barrel.

I stepped a few feet away and lit my smoke. I wondered if it would be possible to pour a bump on my hand despite his savage glare. I didn't think it would be that hard.

"Don't you even think about running, boy."

I decided against the idea.

Every half minute he reminded me he was watching.

I flicked my smoke and got back into the car.

"That's a littering charge to the list."

Fucking cops.

"Your friend hasn't blown under yet," the skinhead cop told me.

I nodded.

"You guys are going to need to get picked up. Who can you call?"

"Can't I just drive?"

"Not if you blow like your buddy," he said. "Besides, get out, see the damage."

I got out.

He walked to the front.

I followed.

The front end was bashed in; both tires were blown and resting on the rims. The windshield was smashed out; that I knew already.

I faked astonishment. "Oh my God," I gasped. One thing I've learned is that if someone of authority is trying to make a point, it's better to be agreeable. The car was still driveable. Shit, we drove it this, far hadn't we? "I'll call for a ride."

"It's a miracle neither of you were hurt."

I wondered why the airbags didn't go off.

The skinhead walked over to the black cop and they started chuckling. Assholes.

I called Matty.

"You sober?" I said.

"Nope."

"Okay, well, act like you are. Robbie and I need a ride."

"Where to?"

I told him. I told him about the cops having us boxed in. He didn't believe me, but said he was on his way.

Robbie and I were standing beside his car. All the cops except the Oreo crew had left. Those two were seated in their cruisers waiting for our ride to arrive.

"I blew twice, over both times, but that guy kept his word."

"I can't believe you told him the truth."

"Who'd you call?"

"Matty."

"Is he sober?"

"Nope."

"Shit."

The tow truck arrived and the cops instructed the driver where to take the car.

The cruisers still had their lights flashing when Matty rolled up. The look on his face as he tried to figure out how to park was priceless. A drunk person trying to make sense of the situation is like the face of a Gremlin after he'd been splashed with water.

"Thank you, officer," Robbie said as we climbed into the Civic.

"You can pick up your licence in the morning," he said. "You're lucky."

Robbie nodded and closed his door.

"What the fuck?" Matty asked.

"Told you," I said. "Let's get out of here."

"Murphy's?" he asked.

"Hell no!" I said reflexively, "Let's head over to Ruby's and drink there."

Ruby's is a one-minute walk from Murphy's.

When we drove past Murphy's, a mountain of glass stood like Lot's wife where the Saturn had been parked.

"I wonder what happened there," Matty questioned to himself.

Robbie smiled, and I admit it, I did, too.

Robbie bought me a beer. He thanked me for having his back and I told him not to think anything of it. He asked me to drive him in the morning to get his licence. I lied and told him I couldn't. I told him I was moving first thing, but really, I wanted nothing more to do with this mess. I knew I shouldn't have called him for the blow. Hindsight is always twenty-twenty; or something like that. I lied again and told him I had to get going. The same way people talk too much is the same way I lie sometimes.

I walked over to Murphy's. Steph was closing up but she unlocked the door for me; not without pretending it was a huge inconvenience.

"You're lucky nobody called the cops."

"I don't know what you're talking about."

She narrowed her eyes and crossed her arms over her chest. She gave me the once over and turned aside to let me in. "Want a beer?"

"Okay."

I drank my beer as she loaded the bar stools onto the bar. We didn't talk about the other week. We didn't talk about tonight. We didn't talk, period.

She flicked off the lights and I knew it was my cue to leave.

"I'm just going to go home," she said.

"Me too." I took the last pull and set the glass on the weathered oak. "Thanks for the beer," I said and stepped outside.

She came out a few minutes later, started her car, and drove away. The beeping alarm box and me in her rear-view mirror.

I was about to start feeling sorry for myself when I remembered the coke in my pocket.

I poured a little bump on my hand and started the walk home.

"Did you tell a black cop that a black man stole Robbie's car, that you found it, and were just driving it home?"

I hung up on Ed.

The clock blinked 7:30.

Some people claim they always wake up a 3 AM because 3 AM is considered the witching hour. It's supposed to be then that the spirits are most active and they boast the ability to feel them moving around in their homes. These types of people really get me going. The nonsense they spout like how they believe themselves to have psychic abilities because once, while they were thinking of someone they hadn't talked to in ages, their phone suddenly rang and it was the person they were thinking of; or if how when they go shopping they want a parking spot close to the mall's entrance, they visualize an open space near the mall's entrance and when they drove up to where they visualized the open space, they found an empty spot!

Fuck. How did I get off on this?

The school counsellor said it was stress.

I don't disagree.

Ms. April, my English teacher, said double negatives destroy good writing.

I think she's wrong.

If I said I agreed I'd be in support of whatever; saying I don't disagree demonstrates that although I'm not in total opposition, I can't fully commit to the idea.

I'm very conscious of the things I say.

I think the counsellor was right in saying my headaches were stress induced, but my stress is different. I'm different. I know how rare that is. I know everybody thinks they're special. I don't think that I'm special, I'm just different and so I expect to be treated that way. You know how everybody thinks they're a great driver? With all those idiots out on the roads, everybody can't be a great driver; well, I am.

Anyway, the counsellor suggested yoga. She said that yoga would help me manage better. All the wheatgrass drinking deodorant opposed hipsters getting together to see what kind of contorted positions they can force themselves into. She said that it would relax me. That it would be good to surround myself with yuppies who believe in chakras and reincarnation and–

Jesus fucking Christ. 7:33 and my mind was already spinning.

People are dumb. And they talk too much.

The counsellor suggested focusing on the things in my life I could control instead of what was out of my control. 7:34.

"You ever been in a sailboat, Troy?" she asked me on more than one occasion. "It's not the wind that determines your destination; it's the set of the sail."

Condescending cunt.

Both times I've been in her office she's pointed to the picture of the yacht framed on her desk and asked me if I'd ever been sailing. Then she recites this atrocious, worn-out example, "The same wind blows on us all, Troy," she'd say, emphasizing Troy while exposing the rodent-like quality of her face whenever she sharpened her eyes to make her point. "What happens, happens to everybody. It's what you do with what happens."

Maybe. But maybe I never wanted to be in the goddamn sailboat to begin with. 7:37.

You know what helps my anxiety? Not yoga. Cocaine. Snow White. 7:38.

And I still had a bag.

.   .   .

For some reason that church song:

> This is the day, this is the day,
> This is the day that the LORD has made,
> We will rejoice, we will rejoice,
> we will rejoice and be GLAD in it...

was playing in my head.

Outside my bedroom window was grey, but it was a joyful grey like on the days leading up to Christmas when everything's still green outside and for no other reason than the feeling, somehow you just know that snow is going to blanket everything right in time for the big day.

Today was Independence Day, not the American holiday/alien flick, my Independence Day; moving day. To celebrate, I poured a gagger, smiled, and even though I didn't believe it, I said out loud, "This IS the day that the LORD has made," and snorted down the entire line.

A text beeped on my phone. It was Jessie.

You up?

It's fucking 8 in the morning. Still drunk, maybe. Hungover, for sure. Newly lit. I laughed.

My dick in a gay bar, I said.

She didn't respond. It's a punchline to a joke I couldn't quite remember.

She said to come over and I told her no.

No response.
I'm moving today, I said finally.
Christen your room later?
Sure.
With that, I got up and showered.

There was nothing in my room I wanted to take with me. I'd sooner light a match to all of it than try and find something to bring with that didn't remind me of here. My clothes, sure. I threw my jeans and t-shirts in the duffel. My books. That's it. The rest of the shit I've accumulated over the years were paperweights.

"Fuck it," I said for my own ears to hear. "Fuck, it."

I picked up my duffel and left my room. Left the house. Started walking.

Christen my room later. Christ.

My grandmother was Catholic. So much so that when I was born, she stole me from my parents. Well, from my dad. My mom didn't see what the big deal was, it wasn't actual kidnapping. Anyway, my grandmother stole me from my dad and baptized me in her kitchen sink. Christened me in her religious tradition. My dad walked in on the ceremony. Me, naked, sitting in one side of the double sink, lukewarm water trickling from the tap down my face.

I was too young to remember, but when I was older, I heard my aunts recounting the story after several bottles of wine. The story went that when my dad walked in and saw this sacrilege, he grabbed his mother-in-law, my late grandmother, and threw her to the floor in order to rescue me from paradise or purgatory or wherever. I'm sure he thought it was a noble act, I mean, his religion demanded it of him, so it had to be, right?

The aunts talked about how they all ran in immediately and found my dad yelling and their mom crying and me wailing. I listened to all this through a vent in the floor from the room I was supposed to be sleeping in upstairs. They drank a lot. They're louder than they think when they drink. One of them said they were sure I'd been cursed. The others cackled and agreed. Cursed. Christened. Shit.

I didn't call Ed. I didn't call Robbie. I didn't call anyone to help with the move. There wasn't anything to move. I hopped on the bus and sat opposite Rosa Parks. That bitch had it all wrong. The back of the bus is the best place to sit.

Carved on the seat in front of me, 'faces sullen clothing grey, walking nowhere walking fast, the people on the street all look sad, but nobody cries anymore.'

People were walking by on the sidewalk. Be it the cloud of the day or the tinted windows or this work of vandalism, the people on the street did look sad. All of them. Their faces sullen. Everybody seemed to be walking somewhere. They were all walking fast.

All of them going nowhere.

What were the chances I'd sit where a graffiti prophet left his mark?

Dimly lit advertisements hung above the people seated on the bus. There was a couple lounging on a bench. They looked sad. Escaping their lives; trying to. The sun kissing their skin. The salt livening the air. It's like they wouldn't even pretend.

I looked around the bus and wondered where these people could be going. The two girls seated near the front, barely old enough to be using tampons, they were obviously going to the mall. Someday they'll grow up to be strippers or teachers or students or junkies. Already they've become conditioned consumers. Everything else is a matter of time.

The lady with glasses sitting to the side, knees together, hands folded neatly on her lap, she's on her way to church or church group or some potluck. She doesn't smile either, though.

The guy in the blue Dickies uniform, his name patch said Red. He's black. Going to or coming from work. Be assured he isn't smiling.

Even the children looked sad, the little girl seated near me at the back of the bus, the one with her headphones on, staring out the window to the gutters filled with trash. I felt sick.

"The people on the street all looked sad, but nobody cried anymore."

It's then I felt my eyes start to well. Leaning back against the corner, I closed them and tried to sleep. It's a forty-minute bus ride including the stop at the main terminal downtown. Sleeping beats crying any day. Still, I felt a creeping warmth, no thicker than a shoelace, slowly making its way down my cheek.

Sometimes I can sleep on the bus, sometimes I can't. Today I couldn't. The goddamn prophet. Goddamn moving. Goddamn cocaine and Jessie and Danielle and all of it.

"Do you ever think about what it was like before all of this?"

No Danielle, I hadn't made it a habit. Now, I couldn't get that damn question out of my head.

Before all of this. Into the chilling past that will never come back. That's from a real prophet.

"When was the last time you visited Casey?"

Fucking Casey.

Fucking Danielle.

After Casey showed up to school with a casted arm, his dad laid off him for a while. Once Casey's arm healed, though, the bruises became a regular accessory. He'd come to class Monday mornings with cuts on his forehead. He'd sport black eyes and fat lips. In gym class you could see the bruises on his thighs.

At first nobody said anything. Teachers turned a blind eye to his beat-up body assuming he was just another trouble maker. By the time you reach high school your size should have forced your dad to think twice before raising a hand to you. For Casey, though, this is when it started. Nobody suspects child abuse at that age. If it's even still called child abuse.

Eventually the bruises assumed Casey as identities always do. If Casey didn't have a bruise people looked at him like they look at someone who switched from wearing glasses to contact lenses. It became that if his nose wasn't bloody or his lip wasn't split, he didn't look like Casey.

Showing up this way earned him a reputation as being a punk. He should have been treated like a tough guy, looking beat up the way he did, like all those guys in *Fight Club*, but he wasn't. Instead of confronting him about his wounds, the kids made up a story. It didn't matter if it was true, it just had to fit. Forget learning in ninth grade science that correlation doesn't imply causation, they had their story, and everybody assumed it was the gospel truth.

Casey Philips liked to run his mouth. It didn't matter how many times he got beat up, he kept running his mouth. The rest is detail.

With a story like this taking root, Casey showing up battered made him a target. It gave everybody in the school a licence to shove him into lockers as he passed by, "When you going to learn, Casey?" they'd say. "It's about time someone shut you the fuck up."

Casey stood five-foot nothing; his figure undeveloped. Unlike most his size, Casey didn't have little man syndrome. He was tame as a little pup, a pup you could carry in Paris Hilton's hang bag.

Ever since I met him, I hadn't heard him lip off or say anything that deserved a smack to the mouth. It didn't matter though. People have the memory of a goldfish and forget everything that happened two seconds before whatever their new focus is.

The story was Casey had a mouth on him and that was that.

Even the adults believed the stories the kids made up. No way a good Christian parent was a belligerent drunk that beat the shit out of him on the regular. Nobody even raised the suspicion.

Teachers simply shook their heads, "Oh, Casey." Like it was his own fault.

You can't imagine the damage this did to his self-esteem. Walking through the halls with his head hung in shame; sitting at the back of class like a leper. Just about every week he'd be sent to the school counsellor for a chat.

"Casey, how do you expect to get along out there if you're always causing trouble? You have to stop acting out."

Casey protested that it wasn't his fault. He pleaded with her that he wasn't going around lipping off or looking for fights. As much as I tried to get him to tell them the truth about his dad being a drunk, he wouldn't.

The only thing Casey was guilty of was protecting his dad; if protecting his dad meant enabling him, then maybe the counsellor was right, and it was Casey's fault.

I didn't mean that. Sometimes when my mind is racing, I end up saying something I never intended.

.　　.　　.

I pulled the cord for the next stop.

After cutting down a side street, I walked down the hill toward the house where I'd be renting the room. The first house I passed was the same as the third house I'd pass which would be different from the next house, but that house would be the same as the second. The neighbourhood looked like something out of a developer's catalogue. Some houses were brick, others sided, some with stucco blasted up and down the walls, but it was obvious there were only three styles of houses to choose from when this neighbourhood was first developed.

Since then, the area has devolved into the ever-sprawling student rental market. A few years back a snake-oil salesman came through town, charging a thousand dollars for his seminar, and promising multiple hundreds of thousands in what they would earn. His secret? Rent to students. Turn your family home into a cash machine. Charge by the room. You can even live in one half while paying down your mortgage on the income generated from the other, have your money work for you. You'd have to be retarded to pass on the opportunity. You're not a retard, are you? It was a grand idea.

This guy had been pitching this strategy for years, his brother or someone had the inside scoop with the Finance Minister or National Bank or whoever sets the interest rate, and he knew that lending rates were going to skyrocket the following year. Most of the people who had just paid the thousand bucks to learn the strategy followed his advice and remortgaged their homes to buy another. The fear of missing out caused a feeding frenzy. Then the economy shifted. The interest rates jumped twenty-five percent and all these first-time landlords couldn't afford the hike. Homes were repossessed. The banks started auctioning their saturated inventory at pennies on the dollar. Guess who swooped in and bought up all the merchandise? All these stupid same-looking houses were now owned by a faceless organization. This is where I was renting a room.

A pine tree towered in the front yard. On two sides of the house, around the second storey, was a deck with a barbecue and patio set. Where a neighbouring house might have been was a park with swings and slides and one of those dome climbing structures with a hundred interconnected crossbars that made it impossible for a kid to avoid smashing his face when he slipped or fell off. The park overlooked the city. I thought that was pretty cool.

I knocked on the front door.

An Indian guy answered. The convenience store Indian not the gas station type. I'd met him when the landlord showed me the house a few weeks before, his name was Mike.

"Hiya, Troy," he said, chin lifted and a gleam in his eyes.

I nodded my hello.

He handed me a key then clasped his other hand on top of mine. "This is your key," he said. "Make yourself at home."

He smiled the smile of people who have taken too many Pollyanna positivity seminars. I could tell we were not going to get along.

A futon bed pressed the wall in the corner of my room. Adjacent to that uncomfortable looking lump was a desk and a small bookshelf. The window didn't have curtains, but being on the second floor it's not like I had to worry about people looking in. There was a shed in the backyard. That was all. If there was a lawnmower in it, I couldn't tell. The yard looked like it hadn't been mowed in ever.

I dropped my duffel on the floor and sat in the chair at the desk. I spun around a couple of times.

The knock on the door surprised me. It was my other roommate. I hadn't met him yet.

"I'm Nate," he said.

"Troy."

"Need a hand bringing stuff in?"

"Nah," I pointed my thumb at the duffel bag. "This is all I got."

Nate looked at the duffel. Paused. Looked back up at me.

"Wanna get high?"

I could tell we were going to get along just fine.

His room was next to mine. Bigger. Much bigger and cluttered with all sorts of objects. Either he travelled a lot and bought souvenirs, or he shopped a lot at the international import stores. He didn't strike me as a yuppie shopper so I assumed the former but I didn't ask.

His bookshelf was filled with books I'd never read, let alone heard of. A rug hung on the wall.

"It's Persian," he said.

His stereo was playing Tool. Their debut album, *Opiate*.

"I love 'Jerk-Off,'" I said. It's a song from the album. I felt like a douchebag as soon as the words left my mouth.

Nate grinned. He opened a tiny box on the shelf above his headboard, shook it, and pinched out two yellow pills. He passed me one.

"Yellow Aliens."

Ecstasy, I'd never done Ecstasy before.

As if I couldn't sound greener, I said, "Let's get high." It wasn't the impression I wanted to make. When did I start caring about what other people thought?

Nate grinned, again.

"You've never done E before, have you?"

I tossed the pill back, winked, and said, "Of course."

We sat listening to his music for some time. We didn't talk. I could feel the vibrations flowing from the speakers. I could see each note as it washed over me. Even the saddest serenades were beautiful. Persians were beautiful. Nate and his blue eyes and messy short blond hair, him and his crooked nose, the way he smiled, all of him beautiful. I caught my reflection in the mirror on the desk. My pupils were dilated, eyes wider than the Red Sea as if my mind had been parted for the first time and I was trying to take in as much as I could. Thirsty and beautiful. I smiled at me.

"Make sure you drink some water."

My head turned lazily to look at Nate. I nodded. A bottle of water appeared in my hand and I took a sip. The water was fresher than any water I'd ever drank. It tasted like a Himalayan brook trickling down a glacier and straight into my open mouth. Someone should bottle this.

Nate was smiling at me. "I have to get to class," he said. He was in university, I think. "Are you going to be all right?"

"Yeah man," I said. "Thanks."

"No worries," he said. "I'll be back later tonight. If you're still up we'll have some brews."

The text said: Ready?

It was Jessie.

Ready, I sent back. Ready for what I wondered. Didn't matter. I was ready. I was really ready. I was as ready as I had ever been in my life. More than ready. And I was throbbing. Jesus was I throbbing.

My phone chimed. She said she was on her way.

I looked at my bed. Where were the sheets?

I walked out of my room and down the hall toward the kitchen. Mike's door was closed but aglow. Beside his room was a closet. I thought the door might lead to Narnia and if it did, I wondered if I'd lose my mind. I froze.

What if Narnia was behind the door? That would be the greatest thing since... I had to open the door.

I placed my hand on the antique bronze knob and turned.

My jaw limped open. Ceiling to floor, wall to wall, stacks of sheets stood waiting. An army of sheets, bright sheets, display case beautiful and Tide clean. I breathed them in, exhaled. I scratched my head. What was I doing in here?

I looked over my shoulder to the open door of my bedroom, saw the naked futon bed and stared a moment Sheets! It needed sheets. What are the chances that I needed sheets and stacked right in front of me were all the sheets in the whole wide world? How good it is to be me.

Delight, that's not a word used often enough. Clean sheets is what delight feels like.

I made the bed.

I pulled a fresh T-shirt from my duffel.

Now, I was surely ready.

I laid back on the bed and listened for the music emanating from Nate's room.

"Californication" by The Chili Peppers.

The knock on my door started me upright. It crept open. Oh, Mary, I thought. Oh, fuck.

Oh. Fuck, fuck, fuck.

Jessie poked her head in.

"Jesus, Troy," she said. "I was standing out front for like twenty minutes."

Oh, thank God, it was only Jessie.

I sighed. "Sorry, baby."

"That Indian guy finally came to the door and let me in... Hey." She snapped her fingers three times. "Are you even listening to me?"

I tilted my head and focused on her lips.

"What the fuck are you on?"

I presented my open palm. "Want some?"

"If it's going to make me as smiley as you, yes."

I pulled her down for a kiss. It was passionate. I spun her around then led her by hand to Nate's room. I took the tiny box from the shelf above his headboard and opened it toward her.

"Indulge, my queen."

Jessie smiled.

"Your wish is my command."

She plucked a pill from the box and tossed it in her mouth like a child would a Pez candy. She was my Pez candy dispenser, head flicked back. A very sexy Pez candy dispenser. I wondered if I could fuck a Pez dispenser.

I returned the box to the shelf.

"Whose room is this?" she asked.

"Nate's."

She didn't know Nate.

Fantastic Planet's, "Stuck on You," was luring me into a trance. The electronic notes inaugurating the grunge that would be the rest of the song paralyzed me.

Jessie was holding an African tribal mask from the lost people of still-shove-animal-bones-through-their-lips-and-strap-gourds-over-their-penises. She set it down and picked up an elephant's tusk.

"Is all this stuff real?"

The song ended and "Dirty Blue Balloons" started playing. I agreed with every word.

Jessie kept talking, I could hear her, but the music overpowered whatever it was she was saying. I assumed she was babbling high.

On the top shelf of the book case, in dark wood, was a hand carved cave man with Rastafarian hair. His cock was thicker than his legs and twice as long. Erect. If women complain that big tits cause back problems, there's no reason this statue shouldn't be crawling.

Jessie stroked the wooden penis. Bit her lip. Walked out of the room.

I followed.

She had me on the bed. We were making out. Every once in a while, she would bite my bottom lip and pull it toward her. This aroused me. She had my belt off. Her hands were down my pants. Then my pants were off; my boxers too.

Jessie bounced off the bed and shut the bedroom door. She resumed her position, only this time her mouth working my cock.

"I want to suck you forever," she said.

"I want you to suck me forever," I echoed.

She worked hard.

I told her I wanted to eat her.

"Then eat me," she said. "But I'm not stopping."

She spun like a bull rider and straddled my face. Her mouth continued to work my centre.

I was hard as I'd ever been. I filled her mouth. She kept sucking.

"Eat!" she commanded, mouth not leaving my cock.

I started with little licks. She dripped. She could have filled a kiddie pool with the amount she was dripping. I started to lap. Top to bottom. I buried my nose in it. I rubbed my face all-around. She moaned moans of Ecstasy.

The love drug.

"Eat," she gagged.

I ate. I bit her lips. I tugged at her clit. I sucked at her skin. God did I eat. She pounded her cunt against my tongue. She rode my face. She grinded on my teeth.

I was about to blow, so I warned her.

"Don't you fucking dare."

I held it.

"You said forever."

I started with my tongue again. Her asshole, so tiny, so tight, looked sweet.

I forced the tip of my tongue inside. Licked. Licked all-around. Jessie was delicious.

Forever, I thought. I could be here forever.

She turned around and mounted me.

Never had sex been so sexual.

Her breasts bounced.

I was mesmerized.

She slapped my face.

.　　.　　.

We lay out of breath for a while. At one point she handed me a lit cigarette. Jessie was good like this. She lit one for herself. The room shook. Her heartbeat drummed her rib cage. Her breath was full. I felt my heartbeat and heard my breath and when my heartbeat and breath became one, I exhaled in bliss.

When we first started fooling around, she wasn't dating her current boyfriend Mitch. She was with Huck. He was another kid from our school and was friends with Ed. One night we were all meeting for drinks and to play football behind the elementary school nearby. Jessie and a couple of the other girlfriends had come along. Us guys were throwing the football around and taking shots of vodka in between.

The girls were perched atop the playground and were taking turns with a carton of spiked lemonade. After it got dark a few of us joined the girls. Huck wasn't one of them. I started chatting up Jessie. She was a little buzzed. Huck was far enough away and it was hazy enough for nobody to make a fuss. I leaned over and kissed her. We started making out. Her hands were on my pants. It was hot. When the carton came around again, we stopped.

That was the beginning.

Ever since that night we'd been getting together, in secret. We'd meet at the beach in the middle of the day while mothers in the water shielded their young kids from us on our blanket. During parties we'd steal off for quickies in the bathroom or an empty bedroom. One time we got away with it at school. That thing how kids are always making jokes about getting frisky in the janitor's closet. It wasn't like that for us. She was a filthy whore, but it didn't mean we had to fuck in filth. We opted for the art department. She was on one of those committees that girls tend to join; yearbook, or cheer, or I don't care, so she had keys. Let's just say there was paint and blankets of paper and the art teacher left wondering who painted such an abstraction. It hung on display for our entire time at the school. Our dirty little secret.

Not really. Everybody knew what we were doing. Well, everyone except her boyfriend. It wasn't supposed to stay a secret. When her and Huck broke up it was supposed to be her and I getting together. We had serious sexual chemistry. We would have been a bombshell couple. Somehow Mitch slipped in and they started dating seamlessly. I was pissed. I didn't want to give up the piece of her I had so we continued on, and still do, and everybody knows except Mitch who knew when it was her and Huck, so he must know now, but like her last boyfriend, is probably lying to himself. I don't get it, I would never let that happen if it was me in his shoes and some asshole was balling my girlfriend blatantly behind my back.

Fuck him, to each their own.

"I love you, Jessie." It felt like the only thing to say.

There was a knock at the door. We jumped. She pulled up the sheets. The door opened slowly. It seemed as if I'd been here before. A head peaked around the corner.

"Put it away–" Ed started. His eyebrows raised with his furtive glance. His lips parted slightly in amusement. "Now look what we have here."

He pushed the door open all the way, a magician making his big reveal. Robbie stood behind him. "I hope we're not interrupting anything," he said.

"What are you guys doing here?" I asked in earnest.

Jessie reached for her jeans. She pulled on her blouse.

"Moving day, buddy," Robbie said. "We've been trying to get a hold of you all afternoon."

"What time is it?"

"Eight."

"Eight? Like at night?"

"Yeah."

I guffawed. "Shit."

Jessie got up, eyes low, and pushed past the guys. Didn't even say bye.

I felt like an asshole. I shouldn't have told her I loved her.

"Wasn't that Mitch's girl?" Ed said.

He knew the answer. I glared. The Ecstasy must have been wearing off. The room was darker than I remembered. Might have been because it was fucking eight o'clock at night. It was still light out, but the room was a shadow. Life was no longer interconnected, I was no more the music than the music was me. It was a terrible feeling. The world truly was a dismal place.

I didn't like how self-conscious I'd become about telling Jessie I loved her.

I do love her. Only not now.

The walls seemed to be closing in. I couldn't breathe. The light faded.

"My uncle just moved in," Casey said.

I knew there was more. "Don?" I asked.

"Yeah."

"Well that will probably be good for your dad, won't it?"

"Maybe."

"What's up, Case?"

"Don." He was unable to speak the words that came next.

"Don? I don't follow."

"I've never told anyone this before."

"I'm not anyone," I grumbled.

"Don raped me."

My face was blank. Casey was serious. He kept his eyes staring at the ground and said it again, "I think he raped me."

"What do you mean, you think he raped you?"

"He raped me."

Casey was more ashamed than sad. His chin dropped to his chest. His eyes remained downcast. "Last summer."

"Why didn't you tell me?"

"I'm telling you now."

By the end of the conversation I wanted to crush the skull of every adult I'd ever met.

"Remember how I went to Golden Lake with my uncle last summer?" Casey said.

"Yeah."

"Then."

"Case, bro, you have to give me more than that," I said, unsure of what to say. "Do we have to kill somebody?"

"Stop," he said. "I just want you to listen."

My nod was weighted with hesitation.

"Last summer," he began, "I was working for my uncle at the Sunrise Greenhouse over on Fourth Street."

"Yeah, yeah. I subbed a few Saturdays with you."

"There. Don always treated us good. He always treated me better. I thought it was because I was family. I didn't know."

"Case."

"Every Friday he let me have a beer at the end of my shift with the older guys."

"I remember."

"It felt good being accepted with them; like I'd made it."

"I was always jealous of you, man." As soon as I said it, I regretted it.

"I know. Looking back, I can see all the signs. I can connect all the dots, Troy. All the flags were there."

In a conversation like this, after you fumble the first few exchanges, you shut up quick, and I did.

"That Friday he mentioned how his cottage needed the roof re-shingled. One beer deep and soaking up the attention from the new group I thought I'd earned my way into, I said, 'I can totally give you a hand.' Hook, line, and sinker, Troy. That was his bait. I remember the other guys in the room. I remember their faces when Don threw the lure out, like they knew his thing for younger boys.

"They winced, Troy. I thought they were avoiding offering their own help. It was awkward. Then to break the silence I said, 'Yeah, for sure. I don't have anything going on this summer; I just have to clear it with my parents first.'

"Do you know how many times I've regretted saying that? Those guys just standing there." His face was dark with pain.

"A few weeks later he was picking me up in his red Tracker at my parent's house. Now every time I see an old Chevy I rage out."

Casey flexed his hands open then closed.

"On the way to his cottage we stopped by this burger shack. Weber's or something. There was a gun warehouse that sold beer right beside. He grabbed a six-pack and wanted to buy me a hat, but I felt like I was already taking advantage of him with the beer, so I said no.

"The rest of the drive up he let me drink. Looking back, I remember asking, 'Aren't you having any?' He told me how it was okay for me to, but that he was responsible to bring me back to my parents safe and sound. He said he'd drink when we arrived.

"At the cottage he showed me my room then pulled out some rum from Jamaica." He paused. He huffed. "I was such an idiot."

I set my hand on his shoulder. "Case." He squirmed out from under my touch.

"He had this handcrafted bar in the living room with mirrors reflecting the collection of bottles. He even had a mirror on the ceiling like you'd see in one of those trashy honeymoon suites. On the counter was a wood carved statue from Thailand or somewhere. Boner. That's what he called it. It was this roughly carved caveman-looking fuck with an oversized erect penis. He laughed when he saw me looking at it. Like I had a choice. It was on the bar right in front of where he stood, so I had to ask about it. He told me his friend who travelled brought it back for him and had a good laugh as he pretended to stroke the shaft. It was uncomfortable, but he's my uncle, so I laughed with him.

"He poured the drinks behind the bar and we went out to his deck overlooking the lake. I felt a little off with the statue and the stroking and the drinks, but him being my uncle and being outside in the woods with the lake, I just sort of dismissed all my concerns."

He clenched his fists and took a deep breath. "I'm such a fucking idiot, Troy."

I watched him silently.

"The people at the cottage next to his were there. A young couple, older than me but younger than Don, they came by when they saw us outside. 'Hey Donny,' the neighbour guy said when they started their walk over. I forget their names but there were two of them and they definitely had their suspicions.

"They drank with us for a while, like that annoying girl who won't leave knowing her girlfriend will sleep with whoever she's trying to save her from. Even if it's not true, I remember their eyes screaming, 'RUN,' but I kept letting him fill my drink. I'd never been so drunk before and it was awesome. The stars out there were fucking outrageous. His neighbours left and we went inside. He poured more rum from behind the bar and then closed the shades. Then he said, 'Fucking Boner, huh?'

"'Yeah Don, that's some weird shit.' I laughed as I drank the new drink. You know how when you're finally accepted, you want to act bigger than you are?"

I nodded.

"I was drinking, trying to keep up because I thought he was drinking just as much as me."

"Case," I said, "we've all been there."

"No, Troy," he snapped. "You haven't."

I bit my lip and dodged his glare.

"Don stood above me and laughed. He said, 'I'm going to suck your dick.'"

Somehow Casey bowed his head even lower and in an almost whisper-like voice said, "I laughed."

I wanted to scream the pause endured so long. I wanted to shake him. I think he wanted me to yell at him and hit him, even though we both knew it wasn't his fault. All it would have been was him bearing the brunt of what we both wanted to exact on the world around us.

"Before I knew it," Casey said, "he was on his knees unzipping my jeans."

"Casey," I said, drawing out his name.

"I was hard, Troy," he admitted. "He gripped it fucking perfectly and then put his mouth on it."

"Case," I said sharply. Casey didn't stop.

"He blew me Troy, and I didn't move. I couldn't move. I just let him suck my dick." Casey scrubbed his eyes, inhaled deep and blew out his lungs. "After a while he took my hands and led me to the bedroom. He laid me on the bed and undressed me. I was immobile. Then he took his clothes off."

"You don't have to do this."

"I felt his whiskers brush against the side of my face. I expected to smell rum on his breath, but there wasn't any to smell. He was stone sober. The whole night had been a set up." Casey picked at his jeans. "He rolled me over. I felt him push against my ass and I knew what he was doing. My face mushed into one of the pillows. I remember seeing an axe in the corner of the room. I remember his dick being soft."

Casey kind of looked up and asked, "Do you remember those water filled worm-like toys?"

I shook my head.

"Water-snakes. That's what they're called. That's what his penis felt like against my asshole. Limp. Trying desperately to force its way in but bending and missing every time he tried. I begged him to stop, I said, 'Don, please,' but this just turned him on more."

Casey burst into sobs.

"It hurt so bad Troy. Like needles being forced through my guts. My body tightened. I could barely breath. It's when everything went black."

He told me how he woke up the next morning to an empty bed. He smelled cooking in the kitchen and could hear bacon frying.

"In the corner of the room where I saw the axe the night before," he continued. "It was gone. From the kitchen I heard Don asking all playful like, 'Is that movement I hear in there?' As if what happened didn't happen. My boxers were folded beside the bed. So were my jeans. I put them on and as I was putting them on, I saw the blood on the sheets."

He shivered.

"I think he went at me all night. I felt like I was going to throw up. The hangover was clawing at the backs of my eyes. 'I made bacon and eggs,' Don said when he saw me. 'I was thinking instead of working on the roof today, we go out on the boat and try and get you up on those water skis.'

"Beside where he was cooking breakfast was one of those old phones with the dials on the front. It was unplugged from the wall. I didn't know what to do. I didn't know what to say, so like the little bitch I am, I said, 'Yeah, that'd be cool.'"

"You're not a bitch, Case. Don't even fucking play that card."

"And that was that. When I called home later that night, Don hovered as I talked to my mom. When it was time for bed, he offered me his, but I politely declined. Can you believe that? I politely declined letting him use me as his sex toy and slept on the couch instead. I barely slept, but I know I dozed off at some point because in the morning he was standing over me again. I just wanted to get out of there. I told him I had to get back to make it on time to watch the football game with my dad.

"On the drive home, we stopped at the same gun shop we stopped at on the way up. I stayed in the car. When Don returned, he tossed a plastic bag on my lap and said, 'You earned it, kiddo.' It was the wide-brimmed hat I was looking at before. I felt like puking. We drove the rest of the way in silence. The fucking guy, he even waved and smiled to my mom when she welcomed me home."

"Casey."

"No, Troy, don't say anything," he said. "I just wanted you to know he was staying at the house now."

"Let's do something about it."

"No."

"He's going to try again."

"I know," he said. "The past three nights he's crawled into my bed after I was already asleep."

"Did you hit him?"

"I went downstairs to the couch."

"Well, I guess that's better."

"No," he said. "He followed me down. I ended up sleeping on the floor."

"Every night?" I asked.

"For the past three."

"Case," I said. "What do you want me to say?"

"I don't want you to say anything," Casey said. "I just wanted someone to know."

The sound of one hand clapping felt an awful lot like Robbie giving me a smack across the face. I looked at him. Starry dots blurred my vision. I thought about saying something, only I didn't know what to say. My jaw limped open like one of those down-syndrome kids in elementary school.

"What the fuck are you on?"

"What?" I looked at Ed. He turned his head slightly to the right, lifted his eyebrows, and shrugged his shoulders.

"It's been a weird day, man."

"You were staring down the hallway after Jessie for like five minutes."

"No," I said, but wasn't sure I hadn't been.

"We've got to get you straightened out."

"Street-note!" Ed snapped.

I don't know when he started doing it, but with increasing frequency he'd just yell out, "street-note" as if he was saying "straighten-out" with a terrible Rastafarian accent.

"Show him."

Robbie pulled a body length mirror from the hall. The type you hang on the back of your door.

My face scrunched. "A mirror?"

"A house warming present," Ed said.

I took it from them and leaned it against the wall. "Uh, thanks."

Robbie flicked something at me. It felt like a rock hitting my chest. I flinched.

"I mean if you don't want it."

I looked down. A chunk of coke lay in my lap. I grinned. "In that case."

With the door locked, mirror laid on the desk, I started chopping lines. I thought about making one giant gagger, end to end, five feet long or whatever the length of the mirror was. Maybe I would have if there had been more coke. Instead I made a single line the width of the reflecting glass. It was still huge and equally a terrible idea. Not because it was a lot of cocaine, the amount never matters. It was a terrible idea because unless you're the one going first someone will always take more than their share. You never cut a single line in a group. You have to divvy them up.

"Dude," Robbie said.

I looked up from the mirror.

"Your sheets are covered in blood."

I looked to the corner of the room and studied the red mess on the futon.

"It's all over your lips, too."

I looked down at the mirror. My lips were red. Lipstick red. Blood red. I stretched them out to see my teeth. They were red, too.

"Fuck."

Both of them started howling.

Ed said, "My boys finally earned his red wings."

Robbie balled up the sheets and threw them in the corner behind the door. "You're an animal."

I split the line into thirds and held up the bill for Ed or Robbie to grab.

Ed declined with the shake of his head. "You go first, buddy. Welcome home."

I grabbed some beers from the kitchen and brought them to my room. There weren't really any spots to sit. Ed spoke for the chair at the desk, Robbie sat on the futon, so I pulled up some real estate on the floor.

"Do you know where to get some E?" I asked Robbie.

"Ecstasy?"

"Yeah, can you get it?"

"I'm sure I can, is that what you and Jessie were doing?"

"You have to try it."

"I don't know, man. Aren't kids dying from bad pills?"

"And I'm pretty sure it will wreck your spine," Ed added.

"I'm telling you right now it's worth the risk."

"What are you still doing with Jessie anyway?" Robbie asked.

"Mitch isn't like Huck," Ed said. "He'll come after you when he finds out."

"If he finds out," I sneered. "Besides, fuck him. If he was anybody, she wouldn't be sleeping with me to get off."

Robbie ran his thumb under his nose and sniffed. "Be careful is all."

"I'm being careful, alright? Can you get it?"

"I'll see what I can do."

"Get ten pills if you can. This shit might be better than coke."

"Fuck off," Ed drawled. "Now you're just tripping."

"Well, maybe they're not comparable, but it sure lasts a hell of a long time. And God, the sex."

.   .   .

When Nate returned from class, he had two of his buddies with him. I didn't catch their names. Both were bigger than Nate, muscular. The one guy looked Italian, olive skin, and his dark oily hair combed back. He wore a gold chain around his neck and a matching, albeit thicker, gold chain bracelet. The type of guy who lifts weights and makes sure everybody knows it. Nate introduced him. I thought about making a Gino joke, but it was my first night in the house and I really didn't want to inaugurate it by picking a fight with some douchebag, so I just shook his hand and offered a relaxed smile.

Nate's other buddy was also a gym rat, but not the type that needs validation from others. This one goes to the gym for his own self-worth and though you can tell he's fit, he doesn't need to show it off. This guy wasn't Italian. I didn't know what he was, only that his name was Jason. He wore a black polo T-shirt and whitewashed jeans. He shook my hand hello and offered me a beer right away.

I think I introduced Ed and Robbie, but can't be sure. The day started with blow, recessed with a little Ecstasy, resumed with more blow and now we were drinking. It didn't matter. Everybody seemed to be having a good time.

"How are you feeling?" Nate said.

"Good, man. That hit was pretty stellar."

Nate chuckled.

"Are you guys drinking with us?" he asked.

"Absolutely."

The Italian douche poured a dozen shots and handed them around. I thought Nate would have led the cheers, some sort of welcome or whatever, but his buddy opened his pie-hole first.

"Salute," he said in a forced Italian accent.

I didn't like the guy from his looks, and now I definitely didn't like him. How people are always saying you can't judge a book by its cover, well, of course you can. That's why books have covers.

We sat around drinking for a while, then Robbie got a call, which I hoped was about the E, and said he had to take off. Ed left with him. Then it was me and Nate, the Douche and Jason; we were wasted.

Mike, who I totally forgot was home, came out of his room once or twice. Each time he did he said something queer like, "Hey guys, I'm trying to study," lips pouty. "Could you lower the volume a little bit, please?" Both times Nate smirked, gave him two thumbs up and a wink, "Sure thing, big guy," and burst out laughing. After the second time Mike appeared, I decided to call it a night.

A bottle shattered outside my room. There was shuffling. I could hear the murmur of voices but just enough to know people were talking, not to be able to make out what they were saying. I laid back on the futon, lights out, and the last thing I remember drifting across my mind was Danielle's question, "Do you ever think about what it was like before all of this?"

It was a Saturday in ninth grade, before the beatings and before Casey had told me about his uncle. We had just made the transition from kings of the hallway as eighth-graders, to lowest on the totem pole as minor-niners in high school. Not that we were ever kings of the hallway but being top of anything and graduating to the bottom of the pile is never gratifying. That and summer was over, so we were no longer able to hang out every day.

This Saturday we'd met behind the Old Mill for some target practice. We were laying side-by-side one spotter, one shooter, passing the pellet rifle back and forth and choosing each other's targets to go for. Casey was usually the better shot, except for today. Today he couldn't hit a bottle if his life depended on it.

I watched his pellet whiz by the cracked Mason jar. "What's up, dude?"

He handed me the gun. I cocked the handle and took aim at the same jar on the ridge. Bottles hung from branches and there were about a million other natural targets to shoot at with all the trees and rocks and birds and squirrels and deer, even though we never shot at birds or squirrels or deer. I focused the sight on the embossed S of the word Mason, exhaled, and squeezed the trigger. The jar collapsed into itself. I handed the rifle back to Casey.

"I've known you long enough to know when something's up."

He took a shot and missed. The pellet didn't even graze the bottle, if he was even aiming at anything.

I sighted in, copied his target, and hit. The bottle chirped but it didn't break. Sometimes the label holds them together, or you need to hit them twice, or I hit too far off centre, so the thing just spun. I put a pellet in the chamber and was about to cock the handle for Casey when he grabbed it from me.

A bird passed above the ridge. Casey aimed high.

We never shot at animals.

He squeezed the trigger. The bird continued its flight.

"We're shooting birds now?"

"Harder than bottles."

"You haven't hit a bottle all day."

"You think you could hit a bird?"

"Fuck off Casey, you know I could, but we don't shoot animals."

"I didn't know you rode such a high horse." Casey never spoke like this. Something was going on that he wasn't telling me.

"Don't be a dick. I'll shoot a bird, but you're going to tell me what the hell's going on or the next thing I shoot is going to be you."

He passed me the rifle. I loaded it, cocked the action, and firmed up my firing position. Then I waited. We waited. There weren't any birds flying near the ridge.

"This is stupid Casey," I said. "Just tell me–"

"There!" Casey pointed. A little blackbird broke the horizon.

I started leading the bird. Hindsight I should have been tailing him; regardless, it wasn't my intended shot so it shouldn't count.

"You're letting him get away," Casey said.

I squeezed the trigger. The bird didn't even chirp; he just fell from the sky. When his limp body thumped to the ground, I dropped my head to the butt of the rifle. Casey didn't say anything. I felt sick.

We left the rifle on the landing and walked to where the bird went down. A dark oily wet spot stained his breast. It trickled down his rigid body. His feet were clenched and tucked tight to his chest. I got down on my knees and whispered, "I'm sorry," more for me than for the bird.

"We have to bury him," I said to Casey.

"Why? Just leave it for the coyotes."

He was right. We'd already... I'd already killed the bird. It would be a worse crime to waste him too. We piled up rocks like an altar. I placed the little dead blackbird on top. I hoped the height would make him more visible from the air and that his scent would be carried farther along the ground.

"I don't feel like shooting anymore," I said. "I don't really feel like doing much of anything actually."

I picked up the rifle and started walking up the escarpment.

"My dad started drinking again."

I faced Casey. I didn't know his dad drank. I'd never seen him drink. Not even when his mom had wine with dinner. I assumed it was because of church and all that.

"Again?"

"My mom left."

My nose wrinkled. "What? What do you mean your mom left? And what do you mean your dad started drinking, again? I've never seen your dad drink even once."

"He used to drink. I don't remember. It was when I was still a kid, but Mom said if he ever started again, she'd leave. He started again. She left."

I rubbed my hands against my forehead to smooth out the ridges.

Casey told me about how when his dad came back from Bosnia, he wasn't the same. I didn't even know his dad was in the army. I guess we don't really know anything about anybody, unless they tell us, and even then, it could all be lies.

I knew Casey's dad did consulting with the military, but I didn't know he served on missions and stuff. Casey said he didn't anymore, that he hadn't since Bosnia. He said the whole thing being a United Nations' Mission meant they weren't allowed to do anything about the injustices they were exposed to. He said because of the things his dad saw, that when he came home, his mind just broke. He hit the bottle hard. Other guys he served with started using heroin. Some committed suicide. He started hitting Casey's mom. This was all before Casey was three years old. Once, his dad beat her up so bad she ended up in the hospital. The police were involved, they took a report, but no charges were laid. Still, it happened. That was her last straw; and his dad's wake-up call. Somehow, they stuck it out. Casey said it was because of the church. Something about divorce being frowned upon and mercy being praised. Casey's dad got sober, him and her they rebuilt their marriage, and for over a decade his dad didn't take a single swig. Until now.

I guess Casey's mom came home to his dad on the back porch tossing beer cans into the yard. Fifteen years sober and then a dozen beer cans littering the yard. That's deep. I used to think those bastards in A.A. were weak because they couldn't quit on their own. I've even taunted some of the saps I've worked with, "Just take a drink," I'd say. "One drink. You're telling me you can't handle one drink?" I guess not.

Casey said his dad's office was trashed. Papers were scattered across the room. The family picture was crushed under the flipped desk. Books were ripped off the shelves. The phone was ripped from the wall.

This is what Casey found when he got home: a mom gone and a dad raging in the backyard. When Casey tried to approach him, his dad swung; something he'd never done before. Casey ran to his room.

And now we're here.

"Where did she go?"

"Who knows, man. Her car was gone. The things from her nightstand were gone. She's gone."

I woke. The room was lit by a midsummer's morning sun at the godforsaken hour of too fucking early. I reached for the clock. My hand flopped through the space where my nightstand should have been. I squinted in agony. I rubbed my face. I scanned the room. A desk, a chair, a small bookshelf, and a window without curtains. My duffel. I wasn't in my room. Well, technically I was, it just wasn't my room from home. I forgot I moved.

I pushed myself to seated and the futon made a terrible metal creaking. I started to laugh. If the bed made this much noise from sitting up, I could only imagine the racket it made when Jessie and I were going at it. Poor Mike.

I didn't think I'd be able to get back to sleep and I had to piss pretty bad, so I got up, steadied myself off the wall, and walked to the bathroom. I pissed fluorescent. Nuclear. I splashed water on my face and looked in the mirror. To my surprise, my face was bright. Under my eyes, the skin was smooth. I smiled. Ecstasy was definitely the way to go.

I looked down the hall and remembered the sounds of the night before. The murmurs, the shuffling, the breaking bottles. With only listening, you can really only guess what's going on behind closed doors. From the bathroom I could see bottles on the floor and the coffee table upturned. I walked closer. The couch cushions were scattered. The TV was muted static. The curtain rod was suspended by one of its hooks. My leg jerked back as a thread of pain pierced the bottom of my foot and shot up my thigh.

"Mother fuck!" I gritted through my teeth.

I thought it was glass. I carefully tilted my foot to see what I'd stepped on and was relieved to find a bottle cap. I brushed it away. These guys had quite the time. Nate was passed out, slumped into himself, mouth ajar, and arms limp by his sides. His snores were roars. Around his shoulders was a frame. A frame that once hung on the wall above where he sat. It used to be a picture of a Matador taunting a bull with a sheet, but now it was pierced by Nate's head and body. The great Matador had finally been slain. Modern art at its finest.

I didn't know where his friends had gone, but I wasn't concerned. If there was a God, they'd have struck a Mac truck on their drunken drive back to wherever they had crawled out from underneath. More likely the two of them were nestled in each others' arms, shit on their dicks and the stale, though remarkably pungent, smell of feces suspended in the air around them.

The kitchen was less of a scene. Bottles were strewn about the counter and a few on the floor, but no broken glass. I opened the fridge to see what I could scrounge. I took a handful of shaved lunch meat and a couple slices of bread to make a sandwich. Whoever's it was, they wouldn't notice.

For once, there weren't any messages on my phone and I kind of felt disappointed looking at it. Sometimes the things we want turn out not to be so great once you get them. I thought maybe I should message the boys to make sure they got home all right. I don't know why I thought I should do that; I just didn't feel as comfortable as I thought I would be being alone.

A voice scratched in the hallway. "Are you kidding me?"

It was Mike. I heard stirring then a slurred speech respond. The response was Nate.

"Are... get outta- Big Guy, you have too uptight," then laughing. What a guy.

"You can be darned sure I'm not cleaning any of this," Mike asserted, possibly more to himself than to Nate. The fridge opened. "Did you eat my lunch meat?"

"Hey," I said. I called Danielle.

"Is everything okay?"

"Yeah, I just thought I'd call. Is that a problem?"

"No, don't be a dick. You just like never, ever, call."

"I was thinking. I wanted to know how you were doing."

"I'm fine. What's up Troy?"

"Do you want to get together later?"

"You're acting very strange."

"Never mind. I was just thinking about you and wondered if you wanted to get together later. Go see a movie or something."

"You know I can't have sex for like six weeks."

"Forget it."

I don't know how long a laid there. I didn't think I dozed off, but when my phone starting vibrating, I jumped up. It was Robbie.

Got it, the text read.

Golden, I said.

Meet at the mall?

Be down there in twenty.

I didn't know it, but Robbie was already at the mall when I arrived. I didn't see his car anywhere so I sat on the bench outside the main entrance. At the far end of the parking lot some douchebag in a black Elantra was blaring heavy metal. It sounded like System of a Down. I checked my phone. There wasn't a text so I decided to wait. The running joke was that Robbie ran on Robbie-time. He was always late. Always. Guess that's why they say behind every joke is a shred of truth. I don't know how he did it, he just did.

I must have sat there for fifteen minutes. I know it was at least fifteen minutes because when I sat down that car was playing "Prison Song," now it was "Chop Suey!" I have the same album. It's a great album. I've probably listened to it a hundred times.

Shit, I thought. The person in the car probably was Robbie. I forgot his car got smashed up.

Fucking guy. For not wanting to draw attention to himself he sure was a heat bag. Sitting there, windows down, *System* up. It was him. I walked over and got in the passenger side. The E was in a little two-gram baggie dotted with purple wizard's heads.

"Blue Starz," Robbie said.

I looked at him quizzically. I didn't know what he was talking about.

"That's what they're called. The colour is the pill. The name is the stamp on it."

I pulled out a pill and examined the thing. Sure enough, there was a little star stamped on each of the blue pills.

"Blue Starz," I said. "You want one?"

"Now?"

"Why not? Trust me, this shit is the bomb."

"What are we going to do?"

"Get high and then drive until something happens."

"Alright."

I pinched one of the little blue pills between my finger and thumb, inspected it, winked at Robbie, and tossed into the back of my throat.

"Bottoms up, big guy."

Robbie popped his, less dramatically, almost apprehensively, and repeated, "Bottoms up."

We drove around most of the afternoon, nowhere in particular, we just drove. Was it Thoreau who said to walk until something happened? I mean we weren't walking; we were driving; well, he was driving, but it had to be close to the same thing.

I stared out the window. The world seemed brighter somehow. It was as if somebody had injected life into the hollow and mechanical grind that was daily living. It was beautiful. The greens were greener. The sky bluer. The people on the street didn't look sad. Everybody appeared to be smiling. Every note that played through the speakers in the car could be felt in stereo. They were warm. They embraced. And they kept moving, flowing beyond. The music was a seamstress sewing everything together. Even the red lights telling us to stop were included in the weave. They were so friendly. They said, "Hey, let's pause for a second. Looks like you needed a rest anyway." God, the stoplights were chill.

I looked over at Robbie, he was thinking the same thing.

When the light turned green, Robbie moved slowly into the intersection and then down the boulevard. Today was going to be a good day. Tonight, would be a good night. The signs were everywhere. A bird winked at me. His wink confirmed what I had just thought. Today was going to be a good day. Tonight, would be a good night.

I didn't recognize my phone's ring when it rang. It felt like all the other music felt. When I realized it was my phone, it was too late to pick it up. The call had gone to voicemail. It was my mom. She never called. Must be important.

It wasn't, or maybe it was. She was calling to tell me I missed my appointment with Dr. Dimock. I'd forgotten all about Dr. Dimock. What a nice guy he was, listening to everybody's troubles just because he cared. I shouldn't have left him waiting for me like that. Poor fellow. Maybe I should get him a bottle of scotch or something as an apology. Hopefully missing the appointment didn't cost my mom anything. It really was an accident. I should call him. Yeah, that's what I'll do. I'll call him. But first I'd have to call my mom, apologize to her, and get his number. Fuck, Ecstasy is great. I think everybody should do it. Imagine world peace? Somebody should write a song about that.

"Everybody should try this," Robbie said.

I smiled.

"Could you imagine all the people,"

"Living life in peace?"

We gazed at each other like lovers.

I didn't recognize my phone's ringer when it rang. It felt like all the other music felt. When I realized it was my phone, it was too late to pick it up. The call went to voicemail. It seemed as if this had happened already.

"Are you going to check that?"

I looked at Robbie. How did he know I was thinking about checking my voicemail? We were telepathic.

"It's a social contract. You have to check your messages when someone leaves one."

He was serious. His eyes bulged.

Robbie reminded me of one of those Nutcracker Soldiers you see around Christmastime. Eyes wide teeth clenched, Botoxed smile, skin taught. I liked Robbie as a Nutcracker Soldier. The tune played in my head.

"Well?" he asked.

"You're absolutely right."

A message is a social contract. If people started breaking contracts all over the place for no good reason, where would society be?

I dialed my voicemail. It was Jessie. She never called. Must be important. It wasn't, or maybe it was. She was calling to tell me something. I couldn't make it out. It was loud and I had to hold the phone far from my ear to hear. Robbie's eyes widened more, as if that was possible. I caught a glimpse of my face and my eyes were saucers. I smiled imagining myself as a Nutcracker Soldier. I saw myself marching to their song.

"What is she saying?"

"I have no idea." I didn't. The sounds were chilling. They rejected embrace. Jessie's words stung. I did not like them.

I pressed the number one to play it again. This time on speaker.

I felt the world being overtaken by a cloud. It was as if the person who had injected life into the hollow and mechanical grind was now extracting it. I pictured a heroin junkie stabbing a needle into an infected vein, pulling back on the plunger to mix blood with the drug. Life was fleeting. The greens were a shade of brown. The sky black. The people on the street were shadows. Everybody appeared to be ghosts. Every note that played through the speakers was an assault. They were sharp. They drilled. And they didn't stop drilling. I felt like they would bore straight through me and into the beyond. The music shackled us together. Everybody. The street lights were mean. "Hey fucker," they swore. "I've got you now." God, the stoplights were scary.

. . .

Jessie was irate. Her words clung together so tightly I struggled to make them out.

"YousunofabichpieceuvshetmutherfuckingphuckTROYy outoremeupyoushreddedmyvaginayoufukkingcaniballlyingas sholeidiotFUCKYOU!" Click.

"Did she say you ripped her up?"

I scratched the back of my head like a dog does for fleas. "I think so?"

"That's hilarious."

"Hilarious? She's pissed."

"I think I'll call you Donkey Cock from now on."

"I don't think it was from my cock, dude."

I remembered being down on Jessie the day before. I remembered all the blood after. I remembered her demanding I ate. I remembered eating. I remembered biting and tearing. I remembered tonguing the tender piece of meat in my mouth and swallowing. Fuck. Had I?

Robbie didn't skip a beat. He pinched the baggie of E between his thumb and middle finger and snapped it open. He offered it to me.

"Have another," he said.

"I don't think having another is going to solve anything."

"Are you kidding me? It will solve everything. Bitches trip all the time. They blow things out of proportion and the only way they feel better about being cunts is to make others feel like shit, too. The only way to win is to brush it off. Don't let it faze you.

"If it was anything serious, she wouldn't have called you in a rage. PMS, guaranteed." He shook the bag like a rattle. "Even if it was a little nick, you two are rough. That and your donkey cock banging the shit out of her; and then us showing up. She's caught being a whore, period arrives, calls you in a rage. They're irrational Troy. Now take one of these blue bits of heaven, and how did you say it, bottoms up?"

Sometimes when you're starting to tumble down a nightmarish rabbit hole, you need a friend to slap you in the face and snap you out of it.

I removed one of the Blue Starz from the baggie. "You're like Socrates, you know that?"

He winked mischievously, "Now one for the Master."

We made our way to the house. I was hoping Nate would still be all fucked up on the couch. I thought it was the funniest thing in the world and I wanted Robbie to see it. That and I wanted to check in with him to see if he was drinking again tonight.

I figured I'd have Ed and Emily over, me and Robbie, him, just get loaded and pop pills and do lines. We could even sniff the Ecstasy. I didn't know if people did that, but since sniffing coke was great, I assumed you could sniff pills and get even more fucked up. Then I remembered Emily didn't do blow, so that would be awkward, but I thought she might try Ecstasy. Everybody should try Ecstasy, so it just made sense that she would at least give it a try. I mean, you can't just knock something without trying it first. I should give Matty a call. Could you imagine if people just made up their minds ahead of time about how they felt about something without ever even giving it a try? That would be stupid.

The house looked innocent. Neat. The bottles had been cleaned up; the broken glass swept, the couch cushions replaced, the curtain rod hung properly on its hooks. Even the framed Matador was hanging on the wall. Well, the frame at least; the Matador was missing. Nate was in the kitchen making a sandwich. He had the bag of lunch meat on the counter.

"Good night, huh?" He laughed. "Can you believe Mike? What a dick coming at me like he did this morning."

I laughed.

"You looked awesome pierced through that frame."

"I was a good time."

Nate gave Robbie the nod and Robbie nodded back.

"Listen," I said. "We were thinking about going at it again tonight. We picked up some pills. I was going to invite a couple people over, have some brews. You in?"

"For sure."

"Cool. Well, rest up, it's going to be wild."

Something about Nate made me keep saying dumb things.

Robbie patted me on the back and smiled.

. . .

I thought about inviting Jessie, just to mess with her into thinking I didn't get her message or more so that I didn't care. Robbie advised me to forget about her.

I'm telling you, Ecstasy made this guy sharp. His exact words, "Fuck her." Genius. I thought maybe we should set up a camera in the room, videotape our conversations and shenanigans.

Again, he had impeccable insight. "Fuck no," he said. "As if you want a video of that floating around out there."

He was right. What if I decided to run for Prime Minister someday? Those types of videos can land people in serious some shit.

"What did you say earlier?"

I had no idea what he was talking about.

"That thing about just going about until something happened?"

"Oh, right. Yeah. Let's just drive until something happens. I think Thoreau said it about walking."

"I like it. Let's do it."

"Sounds good to me."

If one is good, if two is better, three must be best.

This was our logic. It seemed like common sense; and you know what they say the thing about common sense is: "It ain't too common anymore."

We popped a third pill and started driving, half aimlessly, half to get booze and supplies for the night, half because we were high and didn't know what else to do.

"Left, or right?" Robbie asked at the stop sign.

"Left."

I didn't know where left was going to take us, just that left felt good in my mouth. Lef-T. I didn't know if I'd stopped smiling, Ecstasy has that effect, but tonguing 'left' made me smile larger. If that was possible.

On our way, the message read.

I forgot that I'd messaged Ed about coming over. It was starting to get dark. I hadn't noticed before. I'd lost complete track of time. I started to laugh. Robbie and I had done absolutely nothing but drive. Just drive. Robbie must have realized the same thing. He started to laugh.

"That Ed?" he asked.

"Yeah, they're on their way."

"Shit," he slurred. He looked both ways. "We better get back."

"Do you know where we are?"

"No clue. Hard left. I don't think we're too far out of town."

We pulled into a gas station to fill up and turn around.

．　．　．

When we arrived at the house, Nate and his buddies were already going at it. Ed and Em weren't there yet. I texted Ed and he said they were just up the street. They probably didn't leave when he said they did. I don't know why people were always lying. Doesn't matter. We were going to get fucked up tonight.

Nate was on the deck having a smoke. The music from inside could be heard from the street. I wondered where Mike was, but quickly dismissed the thought. Like Candyman or Beetlejuice or someone, I thought thinking about him might make him appear and there's just something about the fun police that grinds me the wrong way.

"I thought you were bringing some friends?" Nate called down.

"Yeah, yeah. They're on their way."

"Cool, well, get your ass up here, let's get this started."

I gave him a salute.

Robbie flushed. "I'm embarrassed for you. You're so weird around that guy. You have to get over yourself."

"Did you guys stop to bang or something?" I said.

Emily's eyes were puffed swollen. She'd been crying. Ed probably said something dumb. I seriously don't know why they've been together so long.

Ed winked.

"We're not all animals," Emily said, face stone. She popped her lips. "I hear you've been going with Jessie again."

I snarled at Ed, "Dude."

"As if I would say anything, Troy. Come on," Emily said.

"Street-note!"

Fucking guy.

"Well," Robbie said. "How about we get a little lit?"

He waved the bag of pills in front of Ed.

"What are those?" Emily asked.

"A gift."

"Ecstasy," Ed said. He rolled his eyes.

"Ecstasy? Like the rave drug? Aren't kids ending up dead because of it?"

Ed gloated. "Exactly."

"Kids are dumb as shit. We've each done three and I don't see any ditches."

"You guys have been doing this all day?" she asked.

"It's probably the greatest drug in the world."

"You guys are fucked," Ed said.

"What's it like?"

"Are you actually thinking about doing it?"

"I might."

"It's the love drug," I said. "Picture the most perfect day, where everything is going your way, the sun is shining, one big long orgasm." I paused. "It's absolute delight."

"Delight?"

"De-light."

"I want delight," Emily said. She presented an open hand. "One please."

Ed slapped her palm away. "I don't think so." He looked at Robbie for support.

Emily would have none of it. "You think you can tell me what I can and can't do?"

They'd definitely been fighting before they came. I hadn't seen the spicy side of her before. I liked it.

Robbie pressed a pill into her palm.

"Just swallow?"

"Just swallow," he said.

Nate and his friends were drunk. They must have started much earlier in the day.

"Who's this little bombshell?" the Italian guy said. This time I caught his name: Joe. Go figure.

Ed's eyes narrowed. He hated people flirting with Emily. I thought he should treat it like a compliment but it always made him mad.

Emily smiled, turned her face to the side, and Shirley Templed a courtesy. "I'm Emily," she said.

He returned her courtesy with a gentleman's bow. "Hi, Emily."

She covered her mouth and giggled.

Ed must have said something really bad for her to be acting out like this. I'd never seen her purposely get Ed amped up. He stormed into the kitchen. Emily stayed with Nate's friends.

"So," Nate said. "Mike was here. He's gone now. I think we should fuck with him a bit."

"What did you have in mind?"

"Oh, you know, piss on his bed, throw his shit on the front lawn, that sort of thing."

"Dude, we can't piss on his bed."

"What, is he your best friend now?"

I didn't really care too much for Mike, still, I didn't feel like harassing him for no reason. I've never liked bullies.

"If you piss on his bed, it's going to smell up our house. Do you really want that?"

"Lame, dude." He sauntered into the kitchen and joined Ed.

"I think we should do another," Robbie suggested.

"Hey Ed," I said. "You coming back with those brews? You wanna pop one of these with us?"

"Fuck no. That shit's for fags."

"Oh, don't be pouty," Robbie said.

He flicked a pill into his mouth and tossed me the bag.

Ed stood in the doorway. I blew him a kiss. He shook his head in disgust.

"If this is what we're doing all night, I'm leaving."

"Don't be like that," Robbie said.

"Are you okay with cheese slices, Master Troy," Nate said from the kitchen.

"What?"

Nate came into the living room with a two unwrapped cheese slices.

"I'm putting these under his sheets."

"Better than piss, I guess."

"How's the trip, Em?" Robbie asked.

"I don't know if it's hit me yet."

"Well, you're grinning like a fool."

"That's because she's sitting next to me," Joe said.

"Fuck you, man!" Ed said, his voice raising an octave.

"Chill," Emily demanded.

"No. I'm not going to chill when this wop is calling me out."

"Who you calling a wop, fag?"

"You want to go, Gino?"

"Are you asking me out?"

Ed lunged at him. Robbie stepped in the way.

"Ed you're being a dick, he's just fucking with you because you're all wound up. And dude," he lamented Joe. "Fuck off. No one's here for a pissing contest."

I watched.

Emily grinned.

Nate came out of Mike's room. "Why is it so fucking quiet in here? Who wants a shot?"

"I'll take one," Emily said.

"That-a girl," Nate said.

I put up two fingers.

"Me too," Robbie said.

"Fuck it," Nate said. "We're all doing them."

Emily leaned over the table where Nate stood pouring. "Can I change the music?"

He pointed to his room. "Have at 'er."

.   .   .

We drank for a while. The Ecstasy must have kicked in somewhere between shots. I was on the deck with Nate and Robbie and Ed smoking. The glow from the city expanded to the stars above. We had the barbecue lit for heat. The Chili Peppers were playing inside. Robbie passed me the bottle. I took a shot, passed it to Ed. The bottle made its way around the circle until it was empty.

"Grab another," Nate said.

Ed stood up. "I'll get it." He went inside.

"He's a fireball, huh?" Nate said.

"He gets a little riled up at times."

Robbie smiled.

Nate looked over the balcony toward the park. He hummed. "So, I gave you your first pill yesterday and now you're hooked?"

"It's a wicked high."

"I know. And you can drink on it forever."

"And fuck like a God."

"I love it," Robbie said.

A bemused smile claimed Nate's face. "You're welcome."

The house erupted with yelling.

"I know what you're doing you wop piece of shit," Ed screamed.

"There you go with wop again. Do you know who the fuck I am?"

"Salami eating Guido wannabe."

"You wish you had a piece a salami half the size of mine."

The crash of bottles came right on cue.

.   .   .

From what we gathered, Ed came in for a new bottle. Joe and Emily were getting fresh on the couch, or so said Ed, she denied it; Joe said they were just talking. But it was enough to send Ed into the red. He flipped the kitchen table. He called Emily a whore. He told Joe he was going to kill him. Emily was laughing. It was the Ecstasy. She was blitzed and didn't care that Ed was pissed. She thought it was hilarious. Thought he was acting the fool and said so. Joe didn't take him seriously either. Ed was drunk. He was slurring his words. He could barely stand straight and had to balance himself with the coffee table.

"We're leaving," Ed said.

Nate's arms were crossed. "That's probably a good idea."

Emily shrugged. "I'm staying."

Ed grabbed at her. Robbie spun him around and looked him in the eyes. "Don't do something you're going to regret."

Ed seethed. He glared at Joe. He glared at Emily. He pointed at her. "I'll be in the fucking car. You'll be out in minute."

She lifted her chin and stuck out her tongue. I got turned on.

"Well that's a drag," I said.

I looked at Emily. She was staring at the ceiling.

"Ah fuck, it happens sometimes," Joe said.

Robbie looked at him. "You're just as bad."

He mock frowned.

"Thanks for the pill," Emily said. "This really is a great high."

Robbie nodded.

I laughed. "You're rowdy."

Emily winked. "Well, I better get going."

"See ya, Em."

She flipped us the bird, "Later, bitches."

Nate went outside, this time with his buddies and a fresh bottle. Robbie and I hung back.

"Well, that was a bust," I said.

"Are you kidding me? That's just Ed being Ed. I'm over it."

"I feel bad for Em."

"Danielle and Jessie aren't enough for you? You want a go at Ed's girl now too?"

"Did I say that?"

"What did you say then?"

"He's pushing the line with how he treats her. Like she's an object. She's actually a really nice girl, and probably too good for a guy like him."

"You'd be better suited?"

"I'm not saying that. I'm saying he's a dick and she shouldn't have to put up with it."

"If she was too good for him, she'd have left."

"That's not fair."

"Oh no?"

"You can't blame her for staying with him. She loves him. She's probably just hoping for the day he stops being a dick to her."

"All I hear is: her fault."

"You know Em. She's a positive girl. An attractive girl. She doesn't just go with anybody. She went with Ed for a reason. He's a reliable dude, and he's probably really sweet to her when we're not around. That'd make it pretty easy to overlook his abusive side."

"Ed's abusive now?"

"It's the truth."

"What's true is you get what you tolerate. Point and match."

"Maybe."

"Let's just drink."

We were posted up in the kitchen drinking beer when Robbie nodded toward the patio doors. "Are you watching this?"

I hadn't been. From where I leaned, I couldn't see outside. "What are you talking about?"

"Your roommate is fucked."

"You should have seen the place the other day."

"No, like fire, fucked."

I started toward the deck. I didn't have to move two feet to see it. On the barbecue, on fire, one of the wicker patio chairs. Nate and his two buddies stood around the flame laughing. Jason had a bottle of lighter fluid. He kept a steady stream on the blaze. Behind the barbecue was the railing. It was wood. The whole deck was wood. No fucking joke.

"We'd better get out of here."

Robbie hummed. His face was pinched. He looked concerned.

We snagged a few shots each and grabbed our beer. Nate stuck his head in when he saw us.

"You guys leaving?"

"Yeah man."

"You don't want to warm up a bit first?"

"Have to bounce."

"But Baby," he said. "It's cold outside." He clasped his elbows and shivered dramatically.

I didn't say anything.

Robbie backed out of the driveway and motored up the street.

"I'm not going to survive a week living here."

"Hopefully you didn't leave anything valuable in your room. You might not have a place to come back to in the morning."

"Fuck."

"Where to?"

"I don't know, call Ed back."

"Because that will be so much better."

"I'll do it."

"You just want Em."

"Fuck off."

. . .

The house was dark when we arrived at Emily's.

"Doesn't look like anyone's home."

"They're out back."

"Don't do it."

"I'm not doing anything. I wouldn't do that. She's Ed's girl. No matter what I think of the situation."

We stalked around the back of the house and sure enough they were sitting under the gazebo listening to music.

Ed noticed us and perked his head up. "Sorry guys," he said. "I couldn't take those goofs a minute more."

"Yeah," I said.

"We get it," Robbie added. "Turns out we couldn't either."

"Oh yeah? What happened?"

Robbie told them about the fire. Emily told Ed to tell us what he did.

"What you did?" Robbie asked.

Ed smiled. "I keyed his car."

"Dude," I said dully.

"Less than a week, man. You were right."

"I think I'd rather be happy than right."

"Well," Ed said. "Fuck 'em."

"Fuck 'em."

"Let's get blotted."

.　　.　　.

One of Ed's good qualities is his ability to play the guitar. The guy moves his fingers like Hendrix. Fuck, maybe that's why Emily has stuck with him as long as she has. Shit, Ecstasy made my mind sharper, too.

Ed always had his guitar close by. This night wasn't any different. At some point the music got turned down and he started playing. Emily signalled for another pill. I slipped her one. She gave me that sexy wink she does. I imagined her sticking her tongue out. Then I imagined her sliding it up and down my cock.

I had it bad. This was bad. Worse than Jessie bad.

Ed was actually a friend.

I bit my lip. Then I noticed Robbie glaring at me.

Ed was oblivious. He was deep into his music.

I held up my hands up in defence.

Emily smirked.

Bad.

I don't remember much past that moment of listening to the music and leering at Em. I was four pills down, and no clue how many shots. That's not counting the beer. What I do remember is Ed poking me in the back of the head. My face was on the table. My hand was on a beer.

"You need to go to bed."

"What?"

"You need to go the fuck to sleep."

I turned my head to the side to look at him. He bared his teeth.

"What's the deal, man?"

"What's the deal? What's the deal, man? Are you fucked?" He slammed his hand on the glass tabletop.

I looked the other way. Emily pouted her lips. I looked at Robbie. He shrugged.

"The deal is you knocked over half the drinks on the table. You soaked my guitar."

"Ed, I didn't mean to do that."

"Yeah, well, it happened."

"Are you kidding? I've seen you feed your guitar beer before."

He glared.

"All right, all right. I'll go to bed. I'm going to finish this beer first though."

"You can crash downstairs on the couch."

I chugged the beer and burped its finality. "Sorry about your guitar."

"Yeah, well."

I found a couple of towels in the kitchen and brought them out for Ed.

"Thanks."

"I really didn't mean to do that."

"All good."

"Thanks for letting me crash here."

.   .   .

The next thing I realized I was on the couch. Must have passed out again. Robbie and Ed were laughing somewhere in the room. One of them threw a blanket over me. I tried to thank whoever but the words wouldn't come out. They laughed again.

"Fucking guy," one of them said.

"You have to admit, he's kind of funny when he gets like this."

That must have been Robbie to my defence.

"Yeah, but don't let him hear you say that, fuck, he might keep it up."

I was onstage. It wasn't a rock concert or stand-up comedy. I don't know what is was or why I was there. Only that I was onstage, lights blinding my eyes, as a roar of applause broke over my ears. Was I in the ocean? No, I was at the beach. Yes, on an island. I woke to the sound and the smell of the ocean. I'd been here before, though not in a while. A light breeze breathed through an open window. The curtain floated with its rhythm. She was beside me, so I kissed her neck. I smelled her hair. I nibbled her ear lobes gently. She was pretending to be asleep, but not really. Smiling, my hands traced her body, the curves, her breasts. She pushed her hips back against my groin and bit her lip at feeling my throbbing.

We started each day this way. Her hand reaching back and guiding me in. Welcoming, moist and gripping. It was making love. She'd wear my shirt into the kitchen, start the coffee, then we'd lay together all morning. Her head on my chest. My arms wrapped around her naked body. Her hair. The smell of her hair. I smiled every time.

Ed's scream started me from my drunken slumber. "You cock sucking mother fucker!"

If I'd have been able to jump, I would have. If I would have been able to jump, I'd have hit the ceiling.

Ed exploded down the stairs and was flying to where I lay on the couch. Where I was pinned down on the couch. Where they had laid me the night before. I remember that. Him and Robbie, they put me to bed. Why was that again? Had there been a fight? Had I hit someone? Something had happened, certainly, but no, maybe there wasn't a fight. I had been put to bed though. One of them put a blanket on me. They were saying something. And then I was... And then I was...

"You fucking whore!"

Emily startled awake. Looked at Ed. Looked at me. I returned the look, eyes demanding, "What the fuck?"

Her face was panicked, but at the same time she looked content. She pushed herself off me. Her hair hung over her shoulders. Her breasts held plump and were firm to her chest. My eyes traced her naked body. Her curves. I could still smell her hair. Her skin.

I smiled reflexively, then remembered Ed.

Emily stood between him and me. She covered her breasts and nestled into his chest. He pushed her away. She ran upstairs, pushing past Robbie who was on his way down. He looked at me and mouthed, "What the fuck?"

I raised my hands.

"Ed," I said. "Brother."

He cocked his fist. "You piece of shit."

My hands were in front of my face, a useless defence if he swung.

I couldn't move. I was wrapped in the blanket. The blanket one of them had put on me the night before. I was wrapped in the blanket. I was wrapped in the blanket!

"Dude, I'm under the covers." I looked down at my clothes. I looked down at my clothes! I was still clothed. "Look, see, I have all my clothes on."

Robbie stood where Emily had, between Ed and me.

Both of them were registering what I was saying. Why the fuck did I have my clothes on? Why was I under the blanket? A naked Emily and I didn't remember any of it. My dream come true and not a memory to boot.

Ed glared ravenously over Robbie's shoulder.

He raised his hand and pointed. "You're a dead man." Then stormed away.

Half way up the stairs, he paused, and said it again, "You're dead."

I sat on the couch, blanket covering my lower half, hands rubbing my face trying to make sense of it all. This was short-lived. I was jarred from my thoughts when Robbie smacked the side of my head.

"What's the matter with you?" I asked.

"The matter with me? Are you kidding? What the fuck's the matter with you?"

"I didn't do a goddamn thing."

"I warned you, Troy. Don't you remember me warning you?"

"I didn't do anything. I woke up to this."

"I saw you at the table last night. You and her playing back and forth the way you were. You're lucky Ed didn't see that. He would have smashed you with a bottle."

"Listen, we were all drunk, high, whatever, the love drug, right? You know what it's like. But I didn't fuck Emily, or lure her down here, or I don't know what everyone thinks. I said I wouldn't do it; I didn't do it. And I have no idea what the fuck happened."

Robbie read my eyes. He was discerning the veracity of my plea. I wasn't lying. I'm pretty sure he could see that.

"Trust me," I said. "I would love to have been there, I mean, damn. But I wasn't. I didn't. I still have all my clothes on. I'm still under the blanket for God's sake. You know if anything had happened that wouldn't be the case. I mean seriously, both of you walked in on me and Jessie before. Did it look anything close to this?"

"Ed's going to be a hard sell."

"I know."

"You should probably duck out of here. I'll see if I can calm him down some. I don't know."

"Yeah. Fuck," I said, then smiled. "Damn though? Did you see those titties?"

Smack. "It's this shit that will screw it for you, man."

I looked him right in the eyes, tilted my head ever so slightly, shrugged just a bit, and let my eyes ask him again.

He smiled. Just a little, "I know, right?"

I folded the blanket and left it on the couch. I had to leave.

"I'm going out the back."

"I'll call you later with an update."

I was closing the patio doors when Ed burst onto the scene again.

"Where the fuck do you think you're going?"

I looked back and caught a flash, a reflection, protruding from his hand.

That thing about fight or flight.

"Jesus, Ed," Robbie said.

The flash in his hand was the bagel knife from the kitchen knife block, each tooth reflecting the light of the room. The blade was at least ten inches long.

"I saw the way you were looking at her last night. I know how you bang Jessie behind Mitch's back."

"Calm down, Ed," I said. Calm down is pretty much the worst thing I could have said. I skirted away from the doors and around the couch. I wanted to keep something between us.

Robbie remained to the side, hands charged but neither in aggression or defence. He stood motionless, yet poised at the ready.

"You're really going to fight me with a knife?"

"You're really going to stand there and tell me you won't fuck anything you want whenever you want?"

Nope, that wasn't what I was going to defend. I do fuck most of whom I want. Except not Emily. Yet. Shit, what's wrong with me?

"Nothing happened, Ed. You know that. I was beyond gone last night."

"Pick up that bottle." He pointed the knife at my empty beer. His eyes were pure rage.

He circled around the couch.

"What I know is that you're a piece of shit and given the chance you'd have fucked Emily."

He had me there.

"Ed, put down the knife," Robbie said.

"Stay out of it," Ed snapped.

I picked up the bottle.

"Ed," I said. "Ed," I repeated.

His eyes stayed on target, on me.

"You and Robbie put me to bed last night. You even tucked me in. I was under the blanket. I was and I am, fully clothed."

"You're not going to talk yourself out of this one."

"Have it your way, but think about this: maybe the person you're actually pissed at is yourself. Maybe, just fucking maybe, if you weren't such a dick, she wouldn't have found her way to me last night."

"Jesus, Troy," Robbie said.

I hit the edge of the coffee table with the base of the bottle expecting it to smash.

It didn't.

With blade outstretched, Ed lunged. I raised my arm in defence. It was a jab. A little stab like I gave Matty. Right in the forearm. My free hand snapped to support my raised arm. "Ed!" I cried. "You actually stabbed me."

"Fuck you!" He slashed again.

I blocked. My arm. His knife. Me and my stupid bottle.

They say if you're ever in a knife fight you have to accept really quick that you're going to get stabbed.

I felt each of the teeth slice through the back of my arm.

Robbie jumped at Ed's arm and wrestled the knife from his grip.

I'd already dropped the bottle and was squeezing where Ed made that last cut.

"Fuck Ed, you got me good." I didn't want to look. Each tooth that sliced through my skin echoed a shadow of pain.

"It's just a little slash."

He knew it wasn't.

"A little slash? Are you kidding me? What in God's name were you coming at me with a knife for anyway?"

"I just wanted to scare you."

"Yeah, well." I uncupped my hand. Blood poured to the floor. I held up my arm for him to see. "Does this look like just scaring me a little a bit?"

Both their faces turned white. Sheet white. Mouths gaped. Neither of them spoke.

I walked to the mirror, arm raised, dripping blood in steps. Down my arm was red. Blood. Down my shirt was red. More blood. Where Ed cut was white. White like Ed's and Robbie's face when they saw my arm white. White like I didn't know why white like. I looked closer. The white was braided. The white was pulsing. No, the white was recoiling. It was breathing. The white was breathing. And then I realized it. The white was the other side of my bicep. The white was my triceps escaping the skin.

Casey glared. "Of course, I want more than this. Did you really just say that?"

"If not this, what?" I was really being a dick. It just sort of crept up on me. I don't know where it came from either. Suddenly I had this overwhelming urge to press him.

Casey didn't say anything.

"Are you going to tell me or did you just say that hoping I'd give you a pass?"

"Why are you being such a jerk?"

"I'm not being a jerk. I'm just sick of it. I don't know how you stay with him, day in day out, and not dream of something better," I said. "Unless this is what you want."

"Screw you, Troy. You're a real dick."

The sun was descending toward the ridge. Darkness was inching close behind. I wasn't angry. I felt at ease with what I had said to him. If he hadn't thought of wanting something more, maybe my prompting would get him started. If he had, maybe my strident remark would be the last kick he'd need to make a change. Either way, I was content sitting beside my best friend, watching the sun settle during this pivotal moment. It was his turn now. I could have sat there all night.

Finally, Casey spoke. "I'd drive," he said. "I'd take whatever I could fit in my backpack and I'd drive."

His eyes began to gloss.

"I've never been west before, so I'd start in that direction. Just drive off into the sun. Race the sunset, windows down, music playing, and leave everything in the rear-view. It would be epic.

"Do you know how big this country is? Even just this area. All the lakes, all the vineyards. I'd let it all flow into the car, into me. All the smells. The sun." He ran his hand through his hair. "I'd play the stereo as loud as I wanted, or when driving through wooded areas, turn it right down and glide through nature listening to the leaves dance in the breeze. Glide so I would see the moose and the caribou and the wolves.

"I wouldn't be in any hurry. Where would I have to be? Some places I might rush through, like the cities, all those concrete jungles radiating heat, not for me. In the grain fields I'd slow down. I might even pull over and watch the harvest. All the giant combines chopping the wheat and spitting it into the trailers they towed behind. A light powder suspended in the air. I'm sure I'd be able to taste fresh bread.

"I'd definitely stop for the trains. Heck, I'd even consider loitering near one of the junctions and hopping on a boxcar as it slowed. That would be an adventure. Just like the *Boxcar Children* I used to read about when I was a kid. I could become a travelling hobo, ha!

"At night I wouldn't get a hotel or bum a bed to sleep in. No. I'd park the car, grab my roll and my sleeping bag, and set up under the stars. I'd sleep in the woods. I'd sleep by rivers and listen to the rushing waters. I'd sleep at the top of hills where I could see for miles around. I could sleep wherever I wanted.

"In the morning I'd wake up with the sun. I'd let the aroma of dew cleanse my mind. I'd eat something simple: fruits, veggies, nuts, beans, seeds. Start the day slow. Nowhere to be, remember? Nowhere to go, except west. I'd get back in my car and run from the sun all morning. I'd watch it in my mirror as it soared into the bright blue sky. And just drive.

"Wait, you know what I would rush to see? The mountains. I've always wanted to see the mountains. I've heard there are even glaciers on some of them. Can you imagine? A glacier. Now that's real history. I don't know what it is about them, but they've always attracted me. How massive they look from far away; I can only imagine how colossal they'd be if I was standing at the base of one. The lakes in the area would all be fed by the melted ancient ice. They'd be emerald green. I'd drink the water."

Casey glowed. I let him.

"Something more, Troy. This is what's more. This is what I'd do. I'd just drive," he said. "For as long as I can remember, in my dreams there's been this voice that's said, 'Go west young man, go west.' Over and over again. I'd just keep driving all the way west. I'd keep listening to that voice: 'Go west young man, go west. Don't stop, just drive. Go west young man, go west.'

"All this bullshit behind me. I'd never turn back. I'd make it all the way to the ocean and set up shop. Get myself a little cabin on the beach. I'd wake to the sound and smell of the Pacific every morning. Slow. Just like I did on the road."

He beamed. Something I hadn't witnessed in a long time. It was an honest smile. Eyes elsewhere, open mouth, scrunched cheeks. He was in his dream. He was no longer that feeble broken kid he'd been beaten into, he was the fearless quirky kid I'd met all those years ago. True smiles are contagious. I know this because for no reason except watching Casey, I was grinning ear to ear.

"And you know what, Troy?" he asked.

I nodded for him to continue.

"You're in my dream."

I cocked my head to allow the thought to settle. What did he mean, I'm in his dream?

Casey leaned over and placed his lips on mine.

I jumped up and pushed him away with both my hands. He fell off the log, dumbstruck.

"What the fuck, Casey?" I yelled. He lay speechless in the leaves. I turned my back to him and started toward my bike.

"Troy!"

I didn't look.

When I was far enough away, but still close enough for him to hear, stonily I said: "Faggot."

. . .

I woke to Emily screaming. Why was Emily screaming? Robbie and Ed were hovering above me. Ed was slapping my cheeks.

"Wake up, buddy. Wake up."

The scene was blurred. The voices of all of the characters from the night before were present, but I didn't know where there was. Was I still at the table? What a fucking nightmare.

"Dude, I must have passed out again,"

Everybody was silent.

I wasn't at the table. They were above me. I was on my back.

Robbie broke the uncomfortable quiet. "We have to get you to a hospital, bro."

"Hospital, I'm fine dude. I'll just sleep it off."

I passed out. It happens all the time. Like every night of the week. Hospital? Why a hospital? Unless. I forced my eyes awake. I looked down at my arm. There was a blood-soaked towel wrapped around my elbow.

"Let's get you up."

Both of them helped me to my feet. Emily gave Ed the car keys.

"You're a fucking asshole," she said.

I was thinking the same thing. I didn't quite feel in the position to admit it though. Fucking guy. I should have balled her last night. What an opportunity missed. Or maybe I did, and I didn't remember. That would be a true shame. One thing for certain, Ed was right, I've wanted to fuck Emily for a long time. I couldn't admit that either.

.   .   .

Anybody who's been to emergency knows there are about three hundred people quarantined in a waiting room, coughing, moaning, sniffling on each other, and often bitching about the wait; rightfully so, because the wait is beyond humane.

I hate hospitals. For the preceding reasons and more. I've never met a hospital attendee who seemed to enjoy their job. I figure if you go into a public service, you should at least enjoy interacting with the public, otherwise, what the fuck? It's worse than the Ministry of Transportation.

The sloth behind the triage window, the first window you go to when you arrive at emergency, asked for my ID and health card. Asked why I had come in today. I saw my reflection in the dividing glass. My eyes were sunken into my skull. My skin was grey. I looked like a junkie. Christ, looking at my reflection made me consider for the first time that maybe I was pushing it a little too hard. How many pills had I popped in the past few days? The coke? The booze? Now this. There was no way she was going to make me a priority. There was no way I could tell her what actually happened.

The first rule above all is never to talk to cops. I don't care if you're in the right, whatever that means. Don't talk to cops. It can never do you any good. And never have them as friends. Period. If I told this ogre that I'd been stabbed before I was in to see a doctor, the cops would have pulled me aside and run their number on me. Then who knows? I'd probably be taken in for questioning and before long I'd be sitting in a cell confused as fuck and wondering if my arm would ever get stitched.

I looked like a goddamn junkie. Fuck.

"You know those aluminum sheds you can buy from Home Depot?"

The lady's mouth limped open under her glassy gaze.

"Well, we were piecing it together this morning and one of the sheets clipped my arm. "I held up my towel wrapped appendage. "It's bad. I'm pretty sure my muscle is exposed."

She scribbled something on her clipboard, then she picked up the next file and began thumbing through it. She looked up, annoyed. "Take a seat, a nurse will call you in shortly."

Robbie went outside to tell Ed we were going to be a while. He was idling in front of the hospital, because apart from being a dick in his relationships, he was a cheap bastard.

Robbie returned ten minutes later, said Ed was going to wait at the coffee shop nearby. We laughed. Then he asked if I'd seen the nurse yet. I hadn't, and told him so.

"Seriously? No one's looked at it?"

"Nope."

"I'm pretty sure you can't stitch a wound after four hours exposed to the air."

"You know what, I think I've heard that too," I said.

"How long's it been?"

"I don't know. How long was I passed out for?"

"Not long. But I'd guess it's been at least two hours since you got poked."

I went up to the window and asked if I would be seen soon, said I was in a lot of pain, and it was getting worse. I lied. I couldn't tell if I was in more pain. I was starting to get worried though.

"People are called according to their need," the cunt said. "Please take a seat, sir, and someone will be with you shortly."

I wanted to reach through the glass and smash her head off the counter. I guess that's why they have the divider in place.

"What'd she say?" Robbie asked.

"That she hasn't been fucked in a while and she wished she could do something about her weight, except Cheetos and Twinkies are just too good to pass up."

"Fuck this place, man. Let's get out of here. We'll stitch it ourselves."

"What do you mean we'll stitch it ourselves?"

"Not you."

"You?"

"No, no. I know someone who can though."

"I don't know."

"We're running out of time."

"You're just tired of waiting."

"No, no. Coagulation and infection and all that."

I pondered this. I had heard the word coagulation before. Didn't have a clue what it meant. Infection on the other hand, I didn't want that. I needed to get this cleaned up.

"All right, call your guy."

I turned a cold eye at the woman behind the glass as we exited the waiting room. She told us we couldn't go out the way we came, and pointed down the hall. I flipped her off.

"Hey," he said. "Are you thinking what I'm thinking?"

"That she's a cunt?'

"No, forget her. I mean about these wheelchairs."

"Like steal them?"

"They're worth a pretty penny."

"How are we supposed to steal them?"

"Like this." He sat in one of the wheelchairs then took off down the hall. "Come on!"

He made it look easy. It wasn't. Me and my one good arm, we struggled. I kept swerving into the wall and had to use my foot to peddle to keep straight.

We rode down the wheelchair ramp outside the doors and then pushed them over the ledge leading to the basement. Stealing them would have been stupid. Destruction, on the other hand, is always brilliant.

.   .   .

Ed was punching his thumbs over his phone when we strolled up.

He looked up. "You're not getting stitched?"

"It's taking too long," I said. "We're going to stitch it ourselves."

"What?"

"Yeah, man," Robbie said. "There's a short window of time you can stitch a wound before coagulation and infection set in."

"Coagulation?"

"Yeah. It's when blood turns to a gel to stop the bleeding. If you clean the wound it's a good thing, but because it hasn't been cleaned yet, it will trap all the shit inside and cause an infection."

Ed and I stared at him. I thought he was bullshitting.

"Where'd you learn that?"

"I don't know, I just picked it up somewhere," he said. "We have to get going though."

"Where to?"

"We'll go back to my house," I said.

"All right, I'll drop you off, but I can't stick around," Ed said.

Good, I thought. I didn't want him around anyway.

Traces of smoke rose from the smouldering mass on the barbecue. I had visions of Nate having burned everything in the house. I wondered why the fire department hadn't been called; or the cops. I was glad the house was still standing.

The smoke clung to the walls and forced water from my eyes.

"It's a good thing we left when we did," Robbie said.

"No kidding."

The living room was twice the display of the first party Nate and his buddies had the other night. The TV was upturned, its screen smashed and glass scattered about the room. The kitchen chairs were missing. There were no books. The fire extinguisher was beside Mike, who was collapsed on the floor under his desk. He was sobbing.

Robbie and I looked at each other, unsure if we should say something. I could only imagine why he was crying. Men that cry weird me out. Men that sob are even worse.

"Uh, Mike?" I said. Robbie made his way to my room.

Mike didn't respond.

"Mike, are you okay, buddy?"

"Does it look like I'm okay?"

Jesus Christ, I guess that's what I get for trying to do the right thing.

"Okay," I said, and started down the hall.

"They burned everything."

I stopped. This was going to be pulling teeth. "One sec, Mike," I said.

In my room I told Robbie I was going to tend to Mr. Melancholy and that there was a first-aid kit under the sink in the bathroom. Whatever else he thought we'd need would be in the kitchen. He said his buddy was on the way. He would have everything set up for when he showed up.

. . .

"All right, Mike, what's the deal?"

"Nate and his asshole friends burned everything."

"I know. They were just lighting the barbecue when we left last night. They can get pretty out of control."

"You were here for it?"

"No. We left when they threw that wicker chair on the flame."

He stopped sobbing.

"I don't know what the big deal is. At least they didn't burn the house down. The rest of the shit can be replaced."

"No, Troy, it can't."

"A few chairs and what? Get up. You're weirding me out."

"You don't get it."

"I know I don't get it, that's why I'm out here talking to you. You don't think I have my own shit to worry about right now? Wonder why my arm's all wrapped up? I came out to check on you, but if you're not going to give me anything to go on, there's nothing I can do."

He looked up. He looked at my arm. "They burned my thesis."

"What?"

"For my Ph.D."

"Like a copy of it?"

"No. Like all of it."

His face was beyond deadpan.

"Don't you have it saved on that big ass laptop of yours?"

I looked at his desk. His laptop wasn't there.

"They burned that, too."

I rubbed my forehead and ran my hands through my hair. I suppressed my laughter. Despite the seriousness of it, I had to hand it to the guys for being so ruthless. Be bold or go home and all that. "Woah."

"I've been here seven years working on that thesis. Nate's always been a dick, but I didn't think he'd ever take it this far."

"Mike."

"What am I going to do?"

"I have no idea, brother," I said. I chortled. "Burn something of his?"

He didn't laugh.

"What happened to your arm?"

"Accident. It's cut pretty bad."

"You should probably go to the hospital and get that looked at."

"That's where we just came from. Taking too long, so we're going to stitch it ourselves."

"Stitch it yourselves? Do you know what you're doing?"

"Robbie has a friend."

"I've got a special sewing kit for stitches. I'll get it for you."

"Thanks. Listen, I'm really sorry about your thesis. If there's anything I can do."

"Yeah, I don't know."

. . .

Robbie's buddy was a dealer, in the same way that strippers said they were only stripping to put themselves through college. He was in medical school. That's how he earned the nickname "Doctor Dave." He wasn't; he just knew how to stitch and did a pretty good job of it. He brought a bottle of Jack Daniels with him. Robbie boiled a pot of water to sterilize the needle and thread. I started cleaning the wound with peroxide, soap, and water. At this point there was no way to get around it.

We convened in my bedroom. I sat on the bookshelf and Doc took the chair. On the desk was the bottle of Jack Daniels, a gram of cocaine, and the first aid supplies.

"What's with the narcotics?"

"You're going to need them," Dave said.

Robbie cut a half dozen lines.

"Take a shot of whisky and two lines."

"Anything the doctor orders."

"Good. Now take another shot and let's get started."

I took another shot.

"Do you know what you're doing?" I asked.

Dave smiled at Robbie; then he smiled at me.

"Give me your arm."

The needle was a fish hook, a large crescent. A foot of black thread dangled from its eye. He wiped away the coagulating blood with the gauze he had pinched to the back of his hand. He looked like a tattoo artist. He probably was a tattoo artist. And piercer. Made sense to me. The smile faded. His straight face made him look uncertain.

"Maybe a shot for the doctor?" I suggested.

He relaxed a little and picked up the bottle. Dave hauled back then passed it to Robbie, who took a shot, and passed it to me.

"Last one 'til we make some headway," Dave said.

He exhaled a sigh that sounded a whole lot like he was holding his breath for the first pass of the needle. He saw the concern on my face and explained that he had to get under the skin but be very careful to keep the needle from piercing the muscle. That I was lucky; it didn't look like there were frays in the braids, and that once it was stitched, it should heal properly, and leave a sick scar. He said that chicks dig dudes with scars.

He thread a couple more passes and asked if I wanted to take a break. I told him no. He said I should at least take another line, keep numb.

I didn't argue.

Doc was cleaning up the desk when my phone rang. I sort of just looked at it, numb from the blow, a little drunk from the whisky, still a little in shock from everything that had been the last twelve hours. I noticed Doc take notice, looked at Robbie, and then Robbie told me to answer it.

"My phone never rings," I said.

"It's ringing."

"Seriously dude, it's a social contract that when someone calls, you have to answer," Doc said.

That was bullshit. I don't have to talk to anyone I don't want to. That's why call display was invented. To screen unwanted calls. But I guess, the truth be told, you never really know who's calling. The screen read Jessie's name. It stopped ringing.

"It was Jessie."

"Fuck her," Robbie said.

The phone started ringing again.

I answered it.

"You asshole!"

"Asshole? That's how we start our conversations now?"

"You ripped me apart."

"What do you mean, I ripped you apart?'"

"At your house. On E."

"I don't think so Jessie." I rolled my eyes. "Actually, now that I think of it, you could have at least warned me you were on your rag. You let me eat you out."

"I'm not on my rag, asshole, that was you!"

"Get fucked Jessie. I'm not in the mood for your dramatics."

"Fuck you Troy. I'm cut up. You did it with your mouth. There's literally no way for me to explain this to Mitch."

"Good, ditch the douchebag."

"You're a real asshole, Troy."

"Yeah, tell me something I don't know."

She hung up the phone.

Doc and Robbie were smirking.

"That sounded rough."

"Did I hear correctly that you ripped her up?" Doc said.

"Some bullshit like that. It's just drama."

"There was a lot, like a lot of blood on those sheets, bro," Robbie said.

"She was on her rag. I don't know what she's going off about. She probably got busted or something and needs to shirk the blame."

"Fuck her."

"Agreed."

"But if you did chew her up," Robbie said.

"I didn't chew her up."

"But if you did," he said. "That's some pretty bad ass shit. Like satanic virgin offering crazy."

"You a Satanist, Troy?" Doc asked.

"If I was a Satanist, Jessie wouldn't have been the sacrifice. The whole virgin thing. That broad has been fucking since she was twelve."

"Let's finish this bottle and call it a night?"

The bottle started its way around. I thanked Dave. He told me to think nothing of it.

I don't remember the guys leaving. I don't remember when I blacked out. Somehow, I'd made it to my bed and now that I was awake, neither of them was around. My head hurt. My nose hurt. My eyes burned. I reached for my elbow to finger the stitching. It was tender. I couldn't bend my arm. Fucking Ed. I should have hit him with the bottle. Maybe it would have broken over his face. Torn his cheek from eye socket to lips. The prick. One thing's for certain though: I am going to fuck Emily now.

I lifted myself to seated. Every movement laborious. I didn't need to be up. I didn't think anyway. I was pretty sure I hadn't made any commitments with anyone or that I had to be anywhere. I thought about calling my mom, checking in with her. She'd be worried with me out of the house and all, lonely. She'd for sure answer the phone. I thought it might be nice for at least a little certainty in the chaos that had become my life. There's comfort in certainty. It is certain my mom would want to talk, and the thought of that sounded comfortable. I don't know. Maybe I'm just a pussy.

I decided not to call her.

Robbie left a note on my desk. It said he'd be by in the afternoon to check on me. Said the lines he left would help me level out this morning. I looked at the lines and contemplated doing them all, quick time, but that wouldn't lead to anywhere productive. Just jonesing for more in about twenty minutes, so I decided to wait.

Maybe I'd skip them all together.

I flipped open my phone to see if there were any messages but the battery had died. I didn't know where my charger was. Nate probably burned it. Ha. No, he didn't. I just remembered his adventure and Mike's laptop and I smiled knowing that somewhere in the madness of it all, there were people whose lives were more fucked up than mine. Maybe it's not me who's so fucked up after all. A reason to celebrate. Celebrations called for cocaine. I sniffed one of the lines and went into the living room in search of

Nate or Mike, but mostly to find a charger that would fit my phone.

I caught a glimpse of myself as I passed the bathroom. I looked at my arm in the mirror. The stitches were tight. It looked good. Doc was right, it was going to be a sick scar.

Nate and Mike weren't around. The smoke still clung to the walls. It's a miracle the fire department didn't get called. I found a charger in the kitchen and brought it back to my room. While my phone was turning on, I huffed another line. I licked my lips. Blinked a few times. All right. Robbie was right. I was starting to level out.

Two alerts. One text. One voicemail. The text was from Danielle. Said she heard there'd been a fight, wanted to know if I was okay.

Fucking people and their talk.

I didn't respond. You get what you tolerate and I no longer tolerated gossip.

The missed call was from an unknown number.

I dialed my voicemail. The message played automatically.

I played it a second time. And then a third. After that third time I set the phone down and rested my head in my hands. It didn't make any sense.

I picked up the phone and dialed Jessie. Voicemail.

I dialed again. Voicemail.

"Jessie," I said. "I think we might have to have a little chat."

I hung up.

I dialed again.

Straight to voicemail.

I slammed the phone on the desk. Pain spiked up my arm. Tears swelled. I looked down at the stitches. Droplets of amber had formed around the thread points.

I took a deep breath. Four lines remained. I opted for two, sat back in my chair, picked up the phone, and dialed my voicemail. I put it on speaker and let it play aloud.

I knew the voice. It was Jessie's boyfriend, Mitch.

"Troy," he said in scathing tone. "I know what you did. I know you raped my girlfriend."

I forwarded the message to Robbie. He called me back in minutes.

"Are you serious?" he said.

"As a heart attack."

"That cunt."

"Yep."

"Like, I don't... It doesn't... Rape? Surely he had to know you two were fucking all along."

"I thought so."

"He knew you were fucking her behind Huck's back."

"He did."

"That bitch."

"I know. But what am I supposed to do? This could be some serious shit."

"Did you call Jessie?"

"Straight to voicemail."

"You know her dads mixed up with the bikers, right?"

"Yeah. Thanks for reminding me."

"No, I'm just saying, maybe we should get out of town for a couple of nights until we can assess the situation. At least until you talk to Jessie. Or Mitch."

"This is exactly what I don't need right now."

"Did you do those lines I left you?"

"Not all of them."

"Well good. Ration them till I get there."

"You're coming over?

"Yeah. We'll hop up to Toronto for the weekend."

"You don't have to do that."

"I could use your help with something anyway. I have to pick up a few things."

"Use my help like last time?"

"I'll be by in a bit. Have a shower. You smelt like shit yesterday."

I divided the remaining lines into four and shot one up the nostril that didn't hurt. It was great coke. I tried calling Jessie again. It went to voicemail after a couple rings. I wanted to kill the bitch. I decided to message Danielle. The worst she ever got was a little dramatic. Drama I could handle. Jessie crossed a line. I knew if I asked Robbie, he'd help me figure out a way to kill her. The cocaine was getting the better of me. I had to switch gears.

I messaged Danielle and told her I was all right. That it was just boys being boys and that Ed and me would be back together again in no time. At least the first part was true. I was pretty sure I was lying about Ed and me ever getting back together. If we did, it would never be the same. Like going back to an ex. There's too much baggage and unreleased blame. There hasn't been any forgiveness or compromise on the issues that initially broke you apart. All I have to do is press my elbow against anything and I'll acutely remember why him and me broke up.

I hopped in the shower before Danielle could respond. I don't remember the last time I showered. It had to have been a couple of days, and with all the beer sweat, hospital, smoke, insert whatever else, and hopefully Emily's vagina residue, the aroma was palpable.

The hot water irritated the cut. I bore the pain; it had to be washed. Especially since I stretched the stitching when I hit the desk.

Rape.

I thought back to our Ecstasy experience. What was it two, three days ago? I seriously had no idea.

I remembered it was very sexual sex.

I remembered being slapped and being turned on by her slapping me.

I remembered her breasts bouncing to almost hitting her chin.

I remembered her mounting and grinding my cock, her hips moving like the swell of the ocean.

I was getting hard. I started stroking myself.

I remembered Matty and whatever he had in his ass. I looked around the shower for something with a handle. There was nothing. I squirted some shampoo in my palm and stroked harder.

I remembered eating her ass.

Her moaning in ecstasy, on Ecstasy.

The way she hoovered my dick with her mouth, opening just wide enough to get her tongue out along the shaft. Her pivoting around to straddle my face so she could keep sucking.

I was close.

My legs flexed. I exhaled.

I remembered her commanding me to eat. I ate.

I sucked at her skin. She was pounding my face with her cunt.

She grinded my teeth as she rode.

I tugged at her clit.

I bit her lips. I ate.

Holy shit.

I hunched as I exploded my passion over the shower faucets.

Holy shit. I thought.

I bit. I ate.

Was it in that order? Did I tear a piece of her off?

It was probably when she was grinding my open mouth.

. . .

By the time I cleaned myself up, Danielle had hit me back. She was happy to hear I was doing okay. I asked her how she was doing. I asked her if she was feeling a little better. The abortion and all. She said she was. She thanked me for taking her to the cemetery. That it was sweet about the roses. I'd forgotten all about the cemetery. Was that really a few days ago? I needed to slow down. I wondered how long I could keep up this pace for. I let that wonder make its way up my nose in two quick huffs.

She asked if I was free on the weekend and if I maybe wanted to get together. My fingers were killing me from all this back and forth. I told her I was busy this weekend, but maybe we could spend some time Monday. She liked that idea. I put the phone down and snorted the last line.

Robbie arrived. He let himself in. I was in the kitchen staring into the fridge for something to eat, even though I knew I wouldn't be able to.

One morning when I was living at home, I'd been lit all night with a couple chasers in the morning to get me straight. It's when my mom came in my room with a stack of French toast. She wanted to surprise me. It used to be our Saturday tradition before things started coming undone. She sat with me while I forced each bite. Eating on blow is like eating cheerios on a summer day with your throat coated in peanut butter. It's impossible.

. . .

"What do you have to pick up in Toronto?" I asked knowing it was probably drugs.

"Blow, mostly."

"Mostly?"

"Yeah, some monopoly money, too."

"Seriously? Liam is out of jail?"

"Just last week. He must have made some moves inside because he's already up and running."

Monopoly money is counterfeit bills. Good counterfeit. Like sometimes even deposited at the bank. We'd take the bills and drive all over the province cashing them in for packs of gum, or cigarettes, or booze. Mostly small purchases to get the most legit change back. Paying two points on the dollar for monopoly is twenty bucks for a hundred. If we had enough funds for ten thousand or more, the price dropped to a point three. Thirteen hundred bucks for ten thousand. That's easy pocket money. I mean, you had to be careful where you passed it off and never to hit the same place twice, and if twice, never a third time. And never to immigrants. Which made it harder because most of the convenience stores were owned by the Indians or the Chinese.

The last time we went on a weekend run, on one of our first stops, the Chinese proprietor realized he'd been taken for a ride and chased Robbie out of the store with a bat. We had a good laugh over that one. A pack of gum with a hundred-dollar bill was ninety-eight dollars cold hard cash.

"How much we grabbing?"

Robbie smiled.

"I got him down to less than a point."

"Jesus. So, what, like a hundred thousand?"

"Exactly."

"Where'd you come up with the money?"

"Pulled it together."

"I want in on this."

"That's why I'm bringing you. Hear anything back from Jessie yet?"

"Nope. There will be consequences though."

"You can bet your pale ass there will be."

The car in the driveway wasn't his Pontiac Grand Am we smashed up, or the Hyundai Elantra rental; today he was driving a white Civic. Except not even this year's model. This baby had to be a few years used. The whale-face for a front end, the Cavalier windshield body, the boxed back end; the kind of car we made fun of kids in high school for driving, even if they earned it, bought and paid for from part time jobs. Don't get me wrong, the car was in good condition. It had stock hub caps and a clean body. I don't know why I was judging his ride like this. I didn't even own a car. But seeing this hunk of shit parked in the driveway made me second guess a weekend in Toronto trying to pick up girls. He had seriously cheaped out on this ride. I thought about calling him on it, but suddenly my mom's voice popped into my head, "If you don't have anything nice to say, don't say nothing."

I didn't say anything. After all, Robbie was doing me a solid bringing me on this adventure. You have to pick your battles, and sometimes you just have to let things go.

It was about an hour drive. Windows down, *System* up. The cool air blew over my face as my ears became deafened by the music and the wind. We didn't need to talk. There was nothing to talk about. We'd been together most every day for the last week. That's the good thing about close friends. Close guy friends. Not chicks. They're always fucking chatting. And if they're not, they think something's wrong and get all twitchy. Fucking bitches. Guys aren't like that. We can sit in silence for hours without uttering a single word.

We passed the canal. We passed where the old burned ship was tied and tilted toward the expanse of the lake. We passed the park where Danielle and I first had sex. The music streamed on. The air blew. We smoked cigarettes. Every so often one of us would reach for the volume knob and turn it up for a song we especially enjoyed. The other would nod his approval. When we hit full volume we laughed, but we didn't talk.

"Are you kidding me Casey?!"

His face swelled above the eyes and lips. The rest was caved in. His skin was checkered blacks and purples. His eyes were blooded. He hung his head. I wanted to beat the shit out of him myself. How could anyone allow this to happen, especially again, and again, and again? I felt how I imagined the kids at school who mocked him felt. How could I respect someone who didn't even respect themselves?

"Are you going to answer me or just stand there all hunched over?"

Casey was crying. I'd never yelled at him before. I didn't know why I was yelling at him now. That's a lie, I did. He reminded me of Old McGregor's dog lying on a nail moaning and groaning but refusing to get up. I was sick of hearing the same story with him clinging to the hope that things would get better. If you want things to change for you, you need to change. That's what my counsellor always told me. Finally, she was good for something.

"Do you want me to hit you? Is that what you'd like? You let your dad do it often enough. Or was it your uncle, faggot?"

I'd snapped. I didn't realize I'd harboured this resentment toward Casey all this time. I don't know if I meant everything I was saying. Surely, I couldn't have. We were best friends. I just wanted it all to stop. And that kiss. I wanted to be the slap in the face to jar him into action. To finally kill his dad, to kill his uncle, to run away, to at least say something. I wanted better for him. I wanted to beat the gayness out of him. How could my best friend be one of them?

"Say something!"

I lurched and pushed him over the log he was standing in front of. He curled up on the rock riddled dirt. I wanted to kick him. I wanted to kick him until he couldn't breathe. No, I wanted to kick him until he fought back. Kick him until I put him out of his misery.

He just laid there.

This entire time I'm raging on Casey, I'm crying. My best friend; innocent, deserving. I hated myself. I hated him for making me do this.

I couldn't believe my thoughts.

Casey wasn't crying anymore, I was. Tears were streaming down my face. They burned my cheeks. My eyes stung. I clenched my fists, my nails digging into my palms. Casey sobbed. He lay fetal on the ground, shaking. My best friend.

"You're just like him, Troy," Casey said. "You're just like my dad. Kick my ass, go ahead. Some friend you are. Did you ever even ask why my dad started drinking again, why he started hitting me? You're just like all the kids at school. Just like all the teachers. You don't care. All I wanted was for you to care. I just wanted one person to be there. Was that too much to ask?"

He stood up and faced me.

"Go ahead, push me again. Hit me. I dare you."

"Fuck you, Casey," I said and pushed him again.

"Good job, Troy. Still won't ask? Don't. You think you're the only person I told about my uncle? Do you think I came to you first? Are you so full of yourself? That's why you never asked. You don't care about anybody but yourself.

"I went straight to my dad. I told him what Don did. I told him about the getting drunk and his brother having his way with me. I told him everything I told you, and guess what? He snapped. He called me a liar. He beat the shit out of me. Not some pussy shoving like you, Troy. No, he let me have it. Called me a faggot. He told me he didn't raise me to be a cock-sucking liar, then he got drunk."

I couldn't believe my ears.

I'd stopped crying. I unclenched my fists. I ran my sleeve across my face and wiped the wetness from my cheeks. I rubbed my eyes.

I took a step back.

No.

I did what I had to do. I did what had to be done. I kicked a cloud of twigs and rocks and dirt and leaves at his face. I spit on the ground in front of him.

"Fuck you, Casey. If you're not going to stand up on your own, I can't carry you any longer. Call me when you do something about your situation."

He didn't say anything. He didn't look up.

I turned around and marched up the hill to my bike.

"Why are we getting off here?" I asked.

We were still a good way out of town and taking the exit for Barton Street in Hamilton.

"The pickup's here. Toronto's just for fun."

"Roger."

"Troy. Listen, I didn't tell you before, but I figure now that we're here you should have full disclosure."

A vein pulsed in my forehead. I glared at him waiting for the rest of it.

"This isn't a rental car."

"Who's is it then?"

"I don't know. It's off my cousin's lot. The plates are... uh, borrowed."

"You've got to be shitting me."

"There's no way I was going to pick up this much shit in a car registered in my name. If we have to, if anything goes wrong, I can't have it tied back to me."

I took a deep breath, a breath so deep it stretched the stitching in my arm. My face winced. Robbie redirected his gaze to the road ahead of us.

We didn't speak while I thought about it. It made sense. Still, I'd rather have known first, but if he told me first, I probably wouldn't have come. Though I did need to get away for the weekend, and I could use the money. It's not like we were going to be driving around all reckless. At least we never set out to be reckless, so there was no real reason for any cops to be running any plates or stopping us for anything. Plus, it was bad ass.

"Thanks for the heads up."

He raised his fist and I returned the gesture with a tap of mine.

Parked in a 7-Eleven parking lot, he left me the keys and told me to take the wheel while he was inside. The apartments were above the store. He said if anything went down, I was to have the car started and in gear as he was jumping inside. My heart raced a little at the thought.

Bad ass motherfucker.

I watched the clock while he was gone. The radio was off. No need to attract any unnecessary attention. Each minute dragged like three. I counted the cop cars as they patrolled the street behind where we were parked, each time certain it would pull in and the gig would be up, but they just kept driving. They just drove. I counted three after the first hour. Then I really started getting nervous. An hour, it shouldn't take this long. I started wondering if it had been a setup to jack Robbie's cash. He had a nice chunk of change on him, plus the blow. It wouldn't be hard to imagine Liam setting us up. He probably owed large for the time he spent inside. People who owe large are desperate, and desperate people will take a swing on their own kind. Think of a drowning man in the ocean attacking their rescuer's attempt of recovery. I thought about going up to the apartment. Or calling his cell. Both could be catastrophic if I was wrong. If the guys thought they were getting stood up, who knows what would happen to Robbie. Or me. Fuck. An hour and fifteen. A fourth cruiser passed. Sweat formed on my brow. I was glad I wasn't high. Though I wished I had some for after all this sorted itself out. Yes, sorted itself out. Everything was going to be okay. Liam was just getting Robbie caught up on what went on while he was inside. Probably thanking him for the stuff we sent while he was away. Thanking him for his continued patronage. Liam was a reasonable guy. I was just on edge because of the car, and Jessie, and my arm, and how I'd moved into a jungle of a house. Take a deep breath. I decided to turn on the radio. I hit the power button and jumped back in my seat when the speakers exploded with

Rage Against the Machine. I spun the volume knob as fast as I could. I laughed so not to cry. It's when I noticed Robbie coming down the stairs. He was looking at me with the face I've become accustomed to from him: What the fuck?

I started the car and popped the trunk. He set the bag inside, then climbed into the passenger seat.

He tossed a manila envelope on my lap.

It was thick. Textbook thick.

"Are you kidding me?" I gawked.

"Let's get out of here."

I put the car in reverse and pulled away.

"Where to?"

"We'll boot up a couple blocks and regroup."

I nodded.

"Why'd you have the stereo up so loud when I was coming out? That's the kind of shit that could sink us."

"That was an accident. My bad."

"Figured so much. Listen. You have to hear the story Liam told me."

"Give it up."

"Okay. So, remember that stuff we brought over to his sister's place after he got booked?"

"The grass, and blow, and E?"

"And tobacco."

"Yeah, yeah."

"Well, I thought they were just playing when we packed that condom in the tube and mashed the stuff in. In all honesty, I thought they were just after a free score."

"I thought the same thing."

"Well, Liam said it was legit."

"What do you mean?"

"After we left, one of his friends with a bench warrant showed up." Robbie smiled. "Liam's sister lubed up the condom and shoved it up the guy's ass."

"What?!"

"Seriously. Then she called in an anonymous tip saying where he was holding up and the police came and arrested him."

"That's fucked."

"I know, right? But he got it through and into gen pop. Soon as he met up with Liam, he squeezed it out and delivered the goods."

"That's disgusting."

"Apparently tobacco is worth more than the drugs inside."

"Jesus."

"And listen to this. They pass the drugs to each other through the sewer system."

"I don't follow."

"Apparently, when you want to make a deal, you arrange a time with whoever, and if they're on a floor below you, the guy with the drugs flushes the toilet at the same time as the guy above him and they drop the package in one toilet and it pops out in the other."

"What happens if the guy's above you?"

"What?"

"If the guy who wants the drugs is above you?"

"I don't fucking know, Troy. I was just telling you what he told me."

"It's still pretty sick."

"Of course. He threw in an extra five for you as thanks."

"Five thousand?

"Yeah."

"Sweet."

Robbie took the wheel. We tucked the wads of cash in the visors. I felt like Tony Montana, us driving around with a hundred and fifteen thousand in counterfeit money and copious amounts of drugs in the trunk. We rolled down the windows and took off toward the highway.

"Dude," I pointed ahead.

Out of sight from the main road but now visible from where we were on the ramp, was a blockade of police cars and their respective patrol men.

"Fuck me," Robbie said.

"We can't go through that. They're probably for us. That mother fucker Liam probably kept you up there that long with all his bullshit stories for these bastards to set up."

Robbie didn't say anything.

"Did you tell him we were headed to Toronto?"

He still didn't speak.

"Robbie!"

"We can't turn back."

"What do you mean we can't turn back?"

"They've seen us by now. If we turn back it's a chase. Do you want to go down for this?"

"So just drive through? In a stolen fucking car? With a boatload of counterfeit money and enough drugs to book us both on conspiracy? I wouldn't be surprised if you had a gun under your seat."

"Fuck you, Troy."

"Do you have a gun under your seat?"

"You decided to come along. I told you about the car. You didn't object to the bonus Liam so generously supplied. You understood the risks."

I didn't speak.

Robbie breathed heavy to calm his tone.

We drove slowly around the bend toward the flashing lights.

"When you make a decision, you stick with it. You accept the consequences. If it turns out to be the wrong decision, change it. But you don't bail at the first hurdle."

He was right.

"If you want me to turn around, we will, but that's another decision you'll have to live with, and I'm willing to bet all this cash that the consequences will be far worse versus us continuing down the road and keeping our cool."

I felt like a kid being lectured and knowing he was in the wrong. I hated the feeling.

"You better be as quick on your feet as you were with the 'black man stealing your car' bit."

Robbie shook his head. "Here's hoping."

Four cruisers lined the roadway. Two on each side, lights off. One cruiser in the centre lane way, lights flashing. A small army of police officers waved flashlights in our direction.

Robbie slowed to a stop. I didn't think we were in the same jurisdiction, but I prayed to a God I didn't believe in that it wasn't going to be the same cops that stopped us coming back from the strip club. It took all my restraint to keep my eyes directed away from the bulging visors gripping the stacks of cash.

An officer came to the window and shone his flashlight in both our faces. First Robbie's, then mine. He told Robbie to turn on the interior lights.

I hoped my heart beating in my throat wasn't visible.

"Where you boys coming from?" the officer asked.

Robbie looked straight at the officer.

"Just jumped off the highway to take a piss. We're headed to Toronto for the weekend."

"Guys' weekend?"

"Our ladies gave us the pass. It should be a good time."

The officer laughed in recognition.

"I'm not overly familiar with these parts," Robbie said. "Is there like an accident up ahead or do you think we could sneak around your car and get on the highway from here?"

The officer dipped his head in the window and looked at me. He pulled his head out and returned his attention to Robbie.

The pause coursed terror in my veins. I'd never felt more done-in for.

"Just checking for seat belts."

There was a crackle on his radio. The police officer hushed his response. I felt the sweat forming again. I was boring holes in the back of Robbie's head. If Robbie felt my stare, he didn't show it.

The officer nodded. "Have a good weekend boys. God knows we don't get too many of them."

Robbie laughed.

"Thank you, officer."

Robbie turned off the interior light and grinned at me through the dark.

The officer waddled mechanically to his cruiser. He spoke into the walkie-talkie on his vest. He got into his seat and reversed the car onto the shoulder. He smiled and waved. Robbie followed suit. I lifted my hand in casual disbelief and waved the Queen's TV wave. I started to smile. Wasn't there a song called "Smile and Wave"? Who was it by again?

"Horseshoe, brother," Robbie said.

I applauded with a slow clap. "Do you remember the Headstones song 'Smile and Wave'?"

"I was thinking the same thing."

"We should get fucking wrecked."

"We're going to."

"I could start right now."

"You can reach the bag through the console in the back."

"Let it begin."

I finished cutting a couple gaggers on the back of System of a Down's *Steal this Album!*.

"You're up," I said, passing Robbie a rolled-up bill I pinched from the stack closest to me.

"Is that one of our hundies?"

"Ceremonial," I said. "It's also going to be the first one we spend tonight."

"Dude, we're not passing monopoly in Toronto. It's too heat."

"Yeah, maybe, but we're still using it for this. And let's stop and pick up a case for the road. I'll spend it there."

"I have no objections to here and now. But passing it off ourselves, I don't know brother. Don't you think we've kind of pushed it a little? I mean, just think about it. We have a lot of shit on us. You've got shit to deal with at home. If that Jessie shit blows up in your face..."

"It won't."

"If it does, because cunts are cunts, and we get nabbed passing a fake note... It doesn't seem worth it."

"Fuck, Robbie."

"What?"

"You're right."

"I know."

"Fuck off."

"Just frame it."

"Ha! Do you remember when I did that with the first batch?"

"Didn't your mom snitch you out or something?"

"Yeah. To an electrician."

"Your mom is pretty rad."

"I guess that's one way of putting it. She's out there, that's for sure."

"Ah, fuck it. Let's rip these lines and pick up a case."

"The only one tonight, though."

"That's my boy; now hold it level."

"How about I hold the wheel too?"

"Now look who's the one with all the bright ideas?"

"Even a broke clock is right twice a day."

I rubbed what was left of the coke on my gums and teeth. I rarely did, but after the week that had just passed, I wanted to be as sedated as possible. I unrolled the bill and read the sequence of letters and numbers running along the bottom. I laughed when I read 'LIA' wedged between a few sixes and five-three-seven. Liam could be such a heat bag. First, he put his name into the numbering. Then there's the six-six-six. And five-three-seven was his cell number when he was inside. No wonder he gave us a bonus. These bills were going to get picked up within the week. They were worthless. Well, worthless unless we passed them off quick. But even then, who knew how long this batch had been circulating before Robbie had picked up ours.

I thought of the first time we grabbed a batch. It was in the early days. The old bills with just an iron-on reflective banner in the corner. We each got a single bill with our initials on it. It wasn't a batch. Just a souvenir for the new adventure we were embarking on. That's the bill I framed. That's the bill my mom snitched me for. Not intentionally, of course. In a way I think she was proud. I lived in the basement, and we needed some electrical work done. The panel was in my room. The guy noticed the framed bill on my desk and when he finished his electricity stuff, he came upstairs and asked my mom if I was an entrepreneur or something. I guess most entrepreneurs frame their first dollar. My mom laughed and told him no. She told him I printed it off the computer. I couldn't believe my ears when she relayed the story to me. She said he didn't believe her. I didn't believe her. Fuck. Good intentions, I guess. But even the best intentions never lit the world on fire, right?

Oh man, that was a time though. I remember how we'd gone into the electronics store to buy a scanner. We scanned both sides of the bill then returned the scanner to the store. When the clerk examined the item, she found the bill on the glass and asked if it was ours. Of course, we took it. Jesus, the number of mistakes we made with that first batch. It was fun though, and I guess in a way we were entrepreneurs. But entrepreneurs learn from their mistakes. This, however, was blatant disregard of all the lessons we've learned.

"The money's no good," I said.

"What do you mean it's 'no good?'"

"Did you look at the serial?"

"How does it read?"

"Six-six-six, Liam's name, and cell block."

"You're joking."

"No."

"That's hilarious."

"Hilarious?"

"It's not like we're going to be spending it. We'll sell the batch and pass only the original sequenced ones."

"It was a dick move, him not telling you."

"Dude, the world isn't out to get you. It could have been an accident. He could have given us his own souvenirs by mistake. Or maybe he did it on purpose thinking we'd laugh. There are a bunch of different variables. Enjoy the ride."

Enjoy the ride. I'll enjoy the ride all right. Tonight is the night I get fucked up. Reckless abandon. Pedal to the metal. Burning the candle at both ends. Kicking ass and taking names. And all the other cliche phrases some yuppie spouts when he's about to do something a little edgy. Fuck edgy. I'm going all the way. Fuck Ed. Fuck Jessie. Fuck the cops. Fuck Danielle. Fuck Liam. Fuck Nate and Mike. Fuck them all. Fuck my dad. Fuck my mom. Fuck Casey. I could kill the bastard.

I saw his bike first. It was parked on the mill side of the river. I knew he would be here. It was Saturday and every Saturday meant the Old Mill.

I called out for him. Waited. Called out again. The forest was peaceful this morning. The sun lit the undersides of the leaves as a gentle breeze rustled the branches. The trickle of the brook sounded like a recording. It smelled like the day after a good rainfall, all the dirt washed away, new life growing from the ground; fresh.

A week had passed since the blow up. I hadn't talked to him. I avoided Casey at school. I stayed away from the Old

Mill. I wanted him to come to me. I wanted him to take back what he said about me being like his dad. I deserved an apology. He deserved what I gave him. He's lucky it was all he got.

I knew that was bullshit. When it was all going down, I never thought I was feeding him the same response his dad had when he found out about Don; it felt so visceral. He was right though. I was being like him. It was a fucking peck on the lips. It was nothing. He bared his heart and I stomped it into the dirt. I'm the one who needed to apologize, if he'd even accept my apology.

It must have killed him to have his only friend in the world come down on him like I had. He was right. I was a dick. He didn't need me to press him. He needed me to be a friend, and I failed.

I scanned the area near the landing to see if I could spot Casey. The reflection of the sun off the water caused me to squint. Near the big maple tree, I thought I saw him slumped over. I started in that direction.

I broke into a run as I neared the tree.

The rope was tied to the main trunk above its crook. Casey wasn't moving. The knot under his chin forced his head to hang backward over his shoulders. His arms hung at his side; hands limply open. His feet were on the ground in such a way that his hips splayed to one side, his feet out to the other. One of his shoes had come off in the struggle.

I pressed my shoulder under his armpit to relieve some of the weight. Casey was unconscious. He felt rigid. I fumbled for my pocket knife then slashed at the rope above his head. Casey collapsed to the ground when I'd finally cut through. He wasn't breathing. At least he didn't appear to be. I pounded on his chest. I tried blowing air into his mouth. In desperation I searched for a pulse. I had no idea what I was looking for. I ran up the hill to get a signal and dialed 9-1-1.

With the paramedics on the way, I returned to my friend. Casey's face was swollen blue-grey and bulging around the eyes. His right eye remained open, pupil dilated, his left eye squeezed shut. I tried talking to him. He didn't respond. I slapped his face. He didn't flinch. His skin wasn't cold which meant he might still have some life in him. I kept screaming at him until the medical team showed up.

They told me: He was a small guy. There wasn't enough weight to snap the neck. The branch must have shifted and left him dangling just above the ground. His feet scraping the ground took off just enough pressure to keep him alive. It's a good thing you showed up when you did. Who knows how long he would have lasted?

In the hospital, Casey was covered in a white sheet up to his armpits. The red and yellow tabs on his chest were wired to a switchboard lying on his pillow. Anodes were taped to his torso. Their wires ran to the switchboard too. He didn't open his eyes. His face was swollen red. It matched the burn around his neck where the rope cut in as he thrashed about while hanging from the tree. The breathing machine forced air into his lungs through a textured tube connected to a blue mouthpiece secured by a strap around his head. It wasn't the worst I'd seen him.

He even looked almost at peace.

The nurse said he would never be the Casey I knew. The amount of asphyxiation he'd experienced and then being revived, he'd be lucky to escape the coma. If he did, he'd be put in a care facility for the rest of his life. I asked if his dad had been there. She said only the first night.

Death is a process, not an event. It's simple, but it's not easy. It's simple, all you need to do is cut off the brain's supply of oxygen and death will get you in a matter of minutes. It's just not easy. There are too many variables. Just think of hanging. You have to consider whether to opt for a full suspension or a partial suspension; a standing hanging or a drop variation. Then you worry about the knot. Where on the neck? If the knot is on the left side of your neck, you might miss the jugular; if the knot is on the right, is it going to hit the carotid; or if you line it up under the chin, can you be sure it's going to hit the trachea? Too high on the neck and your skull is going to carry a lot of the weight and you're simply not going to choke; there won't be enough pressure; which means it's going to result in a near-hanging.

Enter Casey.

And what about the rope? Is it going to break under the pressure of your body fighting for its life? What about what it's tied to? Is the branch going to snap? Will a light fixture come unfixed from the ceiling?

Hanging is a fairly reliable method to achieve a successful suicide, if carried out correctly. But there are just too many things that can go wrong, and if they go wrong, if any of these things happen before death, it means survival and permanent brain damage.

What about a do-gooder coming along and interrupting the attempt? Resuscitation will produce a retarded survivor. The doctors are certain about it: interrupted asphyxia causes brain damage.

I should have just let him die; if I'd just stayed away from the Old Mill that one Saturday. Betraying him wasn't enough. Humiliating him wasn't enough. No. I had to sentence him to a life of drooling on himself and shitting his pants. All he wanted was to be freed of the hell that was his life; instead, I condemned him to a life even more miserable than the one he was trying to escape. Good fucking job, *Troy.*

Suicide is simple. But not easy.

The best thing about the little towns you pass on the way to Toronto is they don't have regular business hours for selling beer and liquor. They're still governed by the liquor board and all that, except they sell their booze out of convenience stores, which is super fucking convenient on holidays and nights like tonight. It means later hours.

It also means it's likely a young kid or a single mom is on the register and lacking experience in the counterfeit bill detection department. They're just there to put in their time and are preoccupied with thoughts of the baby-sitter or the deadbeat dad, or if they can get out of work early with the case of beer they stashed behind the store earlier. Either way, it meant we were getting some roadies and smokes on the lam and likely some pocket change to throw at strippers later in the night. What fun. Passing a fraudulent bill to a single mom who probably got knocked up in some drunken indiscretion, then using the change to toss toward the gaping gashes of soon to be, if not already, knocked up single moms dancing onstage in coked-out bliss. Irony doesn't have to be funny to be amusing.

"What are you smiling at?"

"Life, love, and other mysteries," I said.

"All right Socrates," Robbie smirked. "How about you turn some of that philosophizing into action and bust us a couple more lines? We're about at the store and I want to be good and ripped before we start pounding those beers."

"To cut the lines or not to cut; now that's the–"

"Cut the fucking lines."

I pretended to recoil. "Jesus. Yes, Massa."

The coke was rocket fuel. The fluorescent reflection of the linoleum floor strained my eyes. I blinked a couple of times and asked the attendant where the cold beer was. She earned a double take: red lipstick, probably a brunette by rights, but hair dyed blonde with streaks of black–a real Avril Lavigne type. She looked up from her magazine or phone or whatever she had in her lap. She made a point of showing me how annoyed she was at my untimely intrusion into her obviously pathetic existence, and muttered something about the back of the store. She eyed me up and down, debating whether she should waste her time asking for my ID or if she should let this one go. I returned the look, winked, because why not, trying to determine whether she had a kid waiting for her at home or if she was newly pregnant and reading *Cosmo* for tips on how to be a fit and hip mommy. This dance ended as soon as it began and I grabbed a case from the cooler in back. I asked for half a carton of Red's cigarettes, which may have been pushing it, but when you're locked in to a ride, the urge is to hang on for as long as you can. She slapped the cigarettes on the counter and punched the keys on the register.

The moment of truth.

When you're passing counterfeit money, it's best to act as if you're not passing counterfeit money at all.

Before we could get our hands on fake ID, we would manipulate legit ones to make us appear legal age. We'd rub the numbers with toothpicks soaked in acetone and patiently dissolve the coating and ink below. Then we'd stencil in the new number and gloss it over with a top coat of nail polish. We did the same things with pictures. Except we didn't start out this way. Those first ID's were haggard. Picture printed cheaply and coated with a sheet of laminate from the office supply store. They were shit, but just like when you're passing monopoly money, when you're passing off an altered or fraudulent ID, confidence is key. Look like you're supposed to be there, make it routine and don't give it any more attention than you would a library card.

I was busted on one of these early ID's, by a Chinese store attendant. In retrospect it was a good thing because it forced me to up my game and learn new skills, but at the time, it also taught me an important lesson about getting away with things, and the rules governing bobs and weaves.

Deny. Deny. Deny. Act Surprised. Offer to help.

Five steps. That's it.

Simple as one, two, three. Four-five.

When I went into that chink-mart for cigarettes and presented my cardboard cut-out ID, I acted like it was legit. I acted like I did it all the time. He wasn't fooled. He said, I can't accept this. I questioned why, said it was all I had on me, said everybody else did. He showed me a chart with all the acceptable ID's on it. He showed me the one I altered and how it was supposed to look. There were glaring flaws. Enter rules.

No, that's impossible.

I've had this for years with no problems.

You can't be serious.

(Deny. Deny. Deny.)

Wow. This really is a surprise. I can't believe it.

(Act surprised.)

I guess I'll head down to Service Ontario later and see if I can get this sorted out.

(Offer to help.)

In the end I paid for the cigarettes and walked out with new insight and a mission to get my hands on one of those ID charts for the later editions that would soon have to be prototyped.

Deny. Deny. Deny. Act surprised. Offer to help.

Memorize it.

.   .   .

"53.70," Avril said. For reasons unknown she emphasized the seventy.

I smiled, opened my wallet. It's important the attendant sees the contents. Two twenties and the hundred. Flash a subtle look of disappointment and ask with a tinge of humility if they accept hundreds.

She nodded her annoyed approval. I wanted to shove my dick down her throat and gag that feature out of her repertoire. I handed her the bill instead. She ran it under the UV light. I hadn't anticipated that. She ran the bill between her fingers, feeling its texture.

"This bill feels fake."

"What? What do you mean it feels fake?" Deny.

"It feels fake. Not real, genius."

"That's shit and you know it. You ran it under the light, didn't you?" Deny.

"Don't tell me how to do my job. If I think it's fake, I don't have to accept it."

"Listen. It's real. It's probably just new. I got it from the bank this afternoon." Deny.

"I don't know. You look kind of sketchy."

"What? Are you serious? Look. If this is a fake bill, then I'm a fool. Why would I want to put that on you? You look like a breath of fresh air." Act surprised.

She rolled her eyes.

"Seriously. How about this: I'll leave you my number, if your boss won't accept the bill, call me and I'll come back. If there's no issue, you keep the number and call me, I'll take you out." Offer to help.

. . .

"How'd it go?"

"She questioned its feel."

"That's because they haven't been scuffed up yet."

"I know. I'm high. I forgot."

Robbie put the car in drive. "Let's get out of here before she changes her mind."

"I'll cut the lines."

"Yeah, and open me one of those beers, will ya?"

"Should I light your smoke for you, too?"

"Well now that you've mentioned it."

"Eat a dick," I said, then passed him the jewel case. "And sniff this."

We tossed the empty cans out the window. No point adding an open alcohol charge to the buffet of offences we'd be fed if we were pulled over. Every so often I laughed at the thought of how ridiculous life had become. How this week had been. How today unveiled itself. How every single choice I'd ever made in life had brought me to this exact moment: speeding down the highway, wind blowing in my face, cocaine blown up my nose. What would come next?

I felt loose. I felt alive. I thought about the ridiculousness of it all, without resentment, more with amusement. None of it mattered. Fuck, that was a freeing thought. Life is good. Nothing to lose. I can't believe that bitch said I looked sketchy. I pulled down the visor and flipped the mirror open. I laughed. I looked like that bloke off

Trainspotting. The skinny kid that narrates the introduction urging, "Choose life." I'd been choosing life all right. Nobody was going to tell me how to live it. Master of my own domain. This cocaine makes me feel like I'm on that song. Wait, that wasn't my own thought. System was playing on the radio. Killer song. This cocaine does make me feel like I'm on that song. Surreal. That's the life I've been living. Like a Salvador Dali painting. Was he considered a surrealist, or is that what the critics called him? Seems like everybody has an opinion about everybody else. I should have left that girl my real number. I'd show her sketchy. What does that even mean? Rape. I've already been accused of it. Would I rape someone? Could I? I'm sure I could. That would kill my chances with Emily though. I don't think she's the type of girl to go with a rapist. Is there a type of girl to go with a rapist? There must be. All those perverts in jail getting love letters, and marriage proposals, and nude photos from women on the outside. No. What am I thinking? I couldn't rape the bitch. No matter how much she deserves it.

"How close, dude?" I asked.

Robbie didn't answer. His eyes glowered over the steering wheel.

"How close? I need to get out of this car. I'm starting to trip out."

Robbie still didn't answer.

I back handed his shoulder.

"Fuck Troy. What the fuck was that for?"

"Guy, you were gone."

"What do you mean gone. I'm driving, jamming out to System."

"System hasn't played in like five songs."

"You're tripping, bro."

"Yeah, that's what I said. We need to get where we're going and get there quick."

"All right. How about a pick me up?"

"I need to slow down."

"Don't be a pussy."

Blinded by the lights, I fumbled to hand my ID to the bouncer. I vaguely remember hearing him ask Robbie if I was all right and Robbie assuring him, I was. I wasn't. I imagined myself walking a dramatic ketamine induced moonwalk up the road toward the strip club, erecting myself only a few feet from the door before speaking some sort of greeting articulated perfectly in my mind but mumbled and slurred in conscious reality. The cocaine couldn't have been this good. It had to be cut with something, or the rest of the drugs hadn't quite been expelled from my system and they were mixing with each other to create this hybrid creature. Lights streaked. The music flowed through me. I was a black hole consuming everything around me, sucking life from the dead, changing beer into water, wine into water. Whisky even. There was nothing I couldn't handle. My adrenaline surged. I roared.

The bouncer shook his head. He crossed his arms. "Yeah, he's not coming in here."

"Come on, man," Robbie pleaded.

"He's beyond gone."

Robbie clapped me on the shoulder. "He'll be all right."

"I'm just doing my job."

My ears perked up at that one. It was the opening I'd been waiting for. "So were the Nazis you piece of–"

I didn't feel the hit. What I felt was my face scrape the curb as I tried to right myself. I also felt my jaw connect with the road when my first attempt to stand failed.

I started to laugh.

I laughed harder.

"Did you see that fucker swing at me?"

"Get up, Troy. He didn't swing at you."

"What are you talking about, didn't swing at me? He hit me square in the jaw."

"He didn't swing at you. You let go of the wall and fell."

"What? He didn't hit me?"

"No, and now he's not letting us in."

"That's fucking hilarious," I laughed until I coughed. "Where's the car? Let's go somewhere else."

"You've got to level out, bro, or else it will be the same thing everywhere."

"Yeah, yeah. Got it." I reached my hand at him. "Help me up. Let's get out of here."

"How do you always end up so fucked? You're fine one minute and then... Fuck dude."

"Am I bleeding?"

A voice I didn't recognize asked, "What's wrong with your friend?"

"He's fine. Just a little high."

"He looks more than a little high."

"There's blood all over my hands," I whined.

"Sit him on the floor."

"Sit on the floor, Troy."

"Fuck you. Where are we anyway?"

"Sobering you up so we can go out."

"I'm fine. Let's go throw coins at strippers."

"Drink some cola first."

"I don't want cola. I want another line."

"You need sugar."

I raised the instep of the back of my hand to my nose. "I'm just going to do another bump."

The taste of bile is sweet lying in a ditch. It masks the taste of filter-end-smoked cigarettes. It mixes with bit-tongue-blood and has a Jolt-Cola-mixed-with-Red-Bull-tang. How did I end up in a ditch? Did he roll me out of the car? Robbie! I need to get up. I can't get up. Fuck. There's garbage down here. And it's wet. Sleep it off. Yes. Let these eyes close. Drift. Need to drift. Need to let the current pull me out to sea. Wow. The stars are gorgeous tonight. All of us together in the gutter.

The ring around the moon is a perfect circle and the shadows it casts lay on top of shadows already resting. The stars can be seen in-depth which is realization enough to sadden even the most resolved; looking up at the stars is staring into a time that's long since passed and how is anyone expected to move forward if they're always looking back? It has always been this way, and like stars which appear to have existed eternally burn bright until one day they don't, this will, too.

One second, I was admiring the moon and the stars, reflecting deeply after several bottles of wine, battling the melancholy and sadness which accompanies a pursuit such as this, while my shotgun lay on the table with its shells strewn across the room. Next, I awoke, or some semblance of being awake, overtaken by a stark blackness where my eyes were open but no light was coming through. In the chaos of my mind at the end of its tether I could hear voices, familiar voices, but they were far away and muffled by the ringing in my ears. Consoling voices, assuring voices, voices that parrot everything is going to be okay, but if I had known everything was going to be okay, I wouldn't have been feeling this afraid. The ringing wasn't a dinner bell or an alarm clock; it was the dull droning hum of a gunshot echoing inside four walls.

Lying in my own darkness I began questioning: Had I shot someone? Had there been people here? Had I shot myself? Was this what dying felt like? As I lay on the floor in darkness, I felt a hand pressed against my face and another supporting my shoulder. A desperate, sobbing voice attempted to console me. I recognized the voice, but I didn't know where from. Was I in trouble? No doubt I was in trouble. What could be more embarrassing than surviving a *suicide? Or a homicide suicide? I thought of the mess that would have to be cleaned by someone who'd rather not. Blood sprayed on the walls. Blood on the mirror. Pieces of grey matter stuck to the patio doors overlooking the river. The resale value would plummet.*

How come I can't remember? Who are these voices? Why can't I see? I was so aware of my thoughts that laying there was like existing on two planes as I fought to make sense of the question above all questions: why?

Letting go. If this was suicide, years of endless torment were moments away from eternal nothingness. If a criminal offence, there was no escaping it now. Drifting off. Letting go. My ears stopped ringing. All my pain disappeared. If this was death, I welcomed it.

Flashing lights. People looked panicked. Or concerned. Or relieved. Or bored. What are they saying? Lifted. Jerked. Locked in place. There's motion. Movement is life. What a rush.

Spinning in a straight line. Spun. Is that music? The music has a lot of sirens in it. I've heard this song before. Let me go, I want to throw quarters at strippers. I want to get fucking blitzed. How about Acid? You know, LSD. Something I can breathe. I want to be sedated. Give me some of that Kurt Cobain shit.

Fading again, I need to sleep. That's the trick to Ludes man, fucking Ludes. You have to fight the sleep. If you can fight the sleep, you'll have earned the best trip of your life. If you can fight the sleep. Chicks aren't very good at it. Wait a minute? Are Ludes like GHB, that date rape drug? Guys can do it, but it fucks up girls? Exhale. These exhales are laborious. Laboratory. Am I in a laboratory? Where are you taking me? What is this shit all over me? Let me go. Robbie!

In the morning I awoke, and not some semblance of being awake, but actually so, and it was more depressing than anything I'd ever experienced. In the chaos that was the night before, in the dream where I was dying, I had finally found a place that I didn't want to come back from.

I'd become accustomed to waking up in strange places in stranger circumstances, if you can become accustomed to chaos that is. This was something different. My head didn't hurt, that was the first thing I noticed. Not even the backs of my eyes. I felt hydrated; invigorated almost. What a night. A streak of flashing lights. Was there an accident? I was on my back, everything else was a blur. Where was I? I tried to sit up. The skin on my arms and chest pulled with the attempt. The glow from the hallway filtered into the room and reflected off the metal railings of my bed.

I recognized the metronome beeping as my heart, my pulse, or whatever else they measure with sticky nodes and wires that were stuck all over my body. I was in the hospital! But, why? At least I hoped this was a hospital and not some sort of laboratory. Jesus, if I'd been abducted, I'd be done for. Don't be ridiculous. You didn't get abducted. What happened last night? Liam. The strip club. That apartment, I think. A ditch? No. I couldn't have ended up in a ditch. Robbie wouldn't have let that happen. Would he?

I tried to sit up again and this time I was told to just relax. Just drive. To lay back. Everything was okay. You're in the hospital. Someone will be in to see you shortly. You're lucky you were brought in when you were.

I didn't feel lucky. I felt confused and angry. How the fuck did I end up here?

I wanted my mother. I don't know why I wanted her, but I did. I suddenly felt very empty. Very alone and ashamed. Shame is a terrible thing to feel first thing in the morning. I also felt guilty. I wanted my mother to hold me. I wanted to be told it was all going to be okay. I wanted to be wrapped up in her arms and offered a do over. A second chance, like a video game. Life can be a video game, can't it? I wanted a fresh start.

I reached for my phone. My pants were missing. It was cold. Was I wearing a gown? My arm started aching. For fucks sake. Where was my money? I needed to get a hold of Robbie.

"Troy, honey," the shadow in the doorway said.

"Mom?"

"I'm here."

"What are you doing here?"

ANDREW LAFLECHE

"I've been here all night."

I don't know what came over me. Suddenly I became sad, terribly sad. Sadder than I've ever been in all my life. I started to sob. The sobbing became bawling. Laying there, attached to the heart monitor, wearing a gown, in the dark with my mom by my side, a torrent of tears escaped my eyes. They flooded the bed.

When I finally caught my breath, I was curled up in my mother's arms. Soaked. She was crying too. Real, feeling tears, like I hadn't seen in years. Heart to heart. She used to tell me you're not close enough until you feel the other person's heartbeat. I forgot she used to tell me that. I forgot she could feel.

"I'm sorry, Mom."

She hushed my apology, gently. She kissed the top of my head.

"Everything's going to be okay."

And I believed her.

"We were all pretty scared for you last night," my mom said.

"I don't know what happened."

"You don't remember any of it?" Her voice trailed at the end.

"I've been trying to all morning. All I have are bits and pieces."

"You overdosed."

The words rattled around the room until they settled in the silence. Overdosed. I didn't say anything. I've known people who overdosed, but they were all dead. Was I dead? How would I know if I was? Maybe I am.

"They tested you for all types of things, you kept listing drug after drug: Ecstasy, Cocaine, Ketamine, Heroin, MDMA, Ludes. I rode in the ambulance with you. Christ, Troy, as bad as it was, I had to do all I could to keep from laughing. Every time you said Ludes, you'd say, 'Ludes man, effing Ludes.'

I smiled. Even when she quoted things she wouldn't swear.

"It's from a movie."

"You know they tested you for everything you listed."

"And?"

"They only found cocaine and Ecstasy."

"Can I get charged for that?"

"Are you doing heroin?"

"What? No. Why were you in the ambulance with me?"

"Because I'm the one who called them."

Turns out I was ditched after all. Can't really blame the guy. Like the bouncer said, I was beyond gone. That much I remembered. The fucking Nazi. Somewhere in the mix, Robbie switched teams. He drove me back to my moms, except not all the way. He rolled me out a block from her house.

"The detective asked me if you disliked police officers," my mom added.

"Detective?"

"The one who brought you home."

I let my head flop to the side. "I don't remember any of this."

"I guess he introduced himself to you as a police officer, and you went on one of your rants about all cops being bastards or something."

I chuckled, even though it hurt. That sounded like something I would do.

"Why was there a cop?"

"Providence, Troy. Otherwise you may have died. He was getting off shift and saw your friend let you out. He helped get you home, carried you pretty much, the way you were slumped into him. He's the one who told me to call an ambulance."

My phone vibrated. My mom said, "Troy," eyes weighted, pleading. "I don't think you're allowed to use your phone in the hospital." But what she was really saying was, "Don't let them in. Don't let them pull you back. You can start over. You can come home, begin again. Please, Troy, my baby, do you know how close you came to losing it all? How close I came to losing you?"

"We're not in an airplane, okay?" I reached for the phone and scrolled through my messages. The nurse came in and told me I wasn't allowed to have my phone on in the hospital. My mom shrugged and smiled. I hadn't seen her smile in a long time. My eyes burned with tears. What the fuck had come over me? All this crying. It needed to stop. I pressed my lips together and choked back the tears. Before I turned off my phone, I read the two messages I had. One from Robbie, the other from Danielle. Robbie's said he left me in front of my mom's, told me to call him when I got up. Danielle's was about getting together tomorrow? Was tomorrow Monday? I asked my mom and she told me it was only Saturday. I turned off my phone and thought about why Danielle wanted to get together tomorrow instead of Monday. Maybe we would spend the night together. It would be nice to wake up with someone in my arms, or the way I was feeling, to wake up in someone else's arms.

"Are you hungry?" my mom asked.

I hadn't thought about being hungry. Now that I had, I realized I was. I couldn't remember the last time I ate something. How long can a body survive without food, I wondered.

"I'll get something from the cafeteria and bring it up."

"Thanks, Mom."

"Troy," she said and then paused.

"Yeah, Mom?"

"I love you."

I forced a smile. The opposite of what I wanted to do.

"I love you too, Mom."

When I was a kid, I idolized my older cousin Derek. I remember him dating this little firecracker and the three of us going to the park one afternoon. He was pushing her on the swing. I was sitting on top of the slide resting from a game of tag or whatever we'd just played. Sitting and watching my older cousin who I idolized. He was pushing her from the front, her legs spreading around him whenever she moved in his direction. He pushed her from her waist. Mostly.

This one time, instead of pushing from her waist, he let his one hand run over her crotch, lingering the length of the forward swing. She bit her lip. She looked up. Saw me staring. Blushed. Looked down. Still biting her lip, she gave Derek a look like, "Your little cousin is over there; but I liked it."

I must have been hungover. I get especially horny when I'm hung. I imagined Derek's young girlfriend as Emily, and me as Derek, rubbing her vagina in public. I imagined the sex we might have had the night I awoke to her laying naked on top of me. The smell of her hair filled my nostrils. How her beady eyes would have penetrated mine, staring deep into my soul with an understanding, and vulnerability, and a longing that I recognized. Her history riddled with glimpses of my own life. Her gentleness and passion, qualities at some level I wished I had. To be a better man for her. It would have been making love, not animalistic like with Jessie; the cunt.

I get that she was pissed. Coming down off Ecstasy and all that, she was probably feeling a little low. Probably wanted to be held. I can relate. Ended up with her boyfriend. Comforting. Led to getting touchy. I know it. Something about a woman crying instigates an erection fit to burst my Levi's. Maybe he went down on her. Noticed the rawness. He wouldn't have been able to ignore it. Would have sent him into the red. Maybe he even brought up my name. Jessie would have panicked. Or maybe she felt a little vindictive. She'd been busted by Ed and Robbie after all, naked in my bed in my new room at the house. Jessie was a whore. As long as I've known her, she's had a boyfriend and has been banging someone other than him. Namely me, but there were probably more.

Rape. Seriously? Never in my wildest dreams would I think of rape as something I'd claim when I hadn't been. Women are fucked. It's also the only thing they're good for.

Rape. Rape hunt more like it. I think there should be a day where the sport is rape. Take away its illegality. Let men hunt the bitches. Give them a reason to use such a charge.

I might be onto something here.

In conducting this Rape Hunt, we would completely extinguish any level of negativity associated with the word. "Oh, Troy raped you? Yeah, he got me two Rape Hunts ago." I ought to go back to her place, grab Jessie, and rape her on her front porch.

My hard-on tented the gown I was wearing. Even though I didn't feel hungover, I must have been. All those bags of IV's and whatever else weren't enough to trick my brain into forgetting the morning after is a demand to throw a good fucking into someone. Only person around was my mom.

When I was younger, when I first learned about sex, I thought it would be possible to secretly have sex with a woman while she slept. I thought it would be good practice for my first time, that when I made my own woman, I'd know what to do with her.

My mom used to fall asleep on the couch watching movies late at night. I'd always pass by her on the way down to my room. I didn't think it would be difficult to remove the blanket. I didn't think she'd wake up. She was the only woman in proximity. I'm sure if I had a sister, she would have been the obvious first choice. Especially if she was just a couple of years older and newly wearing bras. It wouldn't mean anything. Alas, I didn't have a sister. I had a mom and a grandma. And don't think for a second, I didn't contemplate the latter either. Now, alone in this stupid hospital bed, hard-on and all; fuck me. What the hell am I saying?

"The chicken didn't look so hot, so I got us sandwiches instead."

My eyes had been squeezed shut, but started when my mom returned. "Sounds good. Thanks."

She placed the tray on the nightstand beside me. "Why don't you come home for a few days?"

I reached for the food. "Yeah, maybe."

"Have you ever thought of..." she paused.

"About getting my shit together?"

"I would have used different words."

"I know I've been going pretty hard at it. Have to face the music someday."

"Well, have you thought about getting your shit together then?"

I paused. Only for effect. I had, I'd been thinking about it. I didn't see any other way out of here. Keep hitting it hard and end up dead in a ditch or get my shit together and pull out of this tailspin. The thing about how for things to change for you, you need to change.

"I have. I don't know. Things are just a little messy right now."

"Look around you, Troy."

I didn't look around. I didn't have to. I knew where I was.

"I'll help you get clean if you want."

"I don't have a problem, Mom."

"Troy."

"Seriously. I don't. It's not denial. I like being fucked up. I enjoy being drunk. I love being high." I felt the blood rush to my head. I smiled. My nose began to drip Pavlovian-like.

"This looks like more than that. You could have died last night."

I shrugged it off. "So?"

Tears shot to her eyes. I shouldn't have said that.

"Do you want to die, Troy?"

"Stop using my name like that."

"Well, do you?"

"Do I what?"

"Do you want to take your own life?"

"No, I don't want to take my own life, Mom."

"You can say that, but your actions speak otherwise."

Mom made up the bed in my old room and told me to get some rest. She'd be down to check on me every so often. If I needed anything, to just holler up to her. Asked if I wanted to see visitors if they came by. Said she'd give me my space. She was happy I was home.

When she left, I reached under the bed for Christina Aguilera. I wasn't sure if she'd been swept away when my mom cleaned the room. My fingers brushed the glossy cover and the first thing I thought was how people don't know how to clean properly. They always sweep around the dust bin or vacuum around the couch. They never go deep. Focus on the task at hand. Christina will let me go deep. She was waiting for me to return. At least that's what I told myself. Self-talk to reinvigorate that hard-on. She gets me every time. Her on the cover in that white swimsuit, topless. The picture of her floating in the ocean. Her lying in the sand. Of course, the one that always does it for me is the one of her standing by the water, one hand cupping her breasts, the other giving me the finger.

Only it didn't get me this time.

I threw the magazine across the room.

Things were different. Whether I wanted them to be or not. Something had changed.

. . .

It must have been later that day, or maybe it was one of the subsequent. Whenever it was, visitors finally arrived, and when they did, it was Ed and Robbie. They had a grocery bag with them. Said it was a get-well package and threw it at me.

Robbie smiled with mischief. "To help with your recovery."

I untied the bag and fingered my way through the contents. There was an envelope of cash, the funny money. Some DVDs. And a bag of what looked like mushrooms. Surely, they knew better than to bring me hallucinogenics having just got out of the hospital for over indulging in pharmaceuticals and all.

"This is a joke, right? Mushrooms?"

"Nature's medicine."

"I haven't done mushrooms in forever. I don't even know if I could handle them right now. Look at me."

Ed's face twisted and he moved a little closer like he was inspecting something. "Are you still wearing the hospital anodes?"

I looked down. I'd forgot about them. "Maybe I could use a few caps after all. They might level me out."

I tossed a handful of stems into my mouth and chewed. They tasted like shit. They tasted like shit because mushrooms are grown in shit.

"I can't believe you just ate those," Ed said. "You've got a problem, Troy. You just got out of the hospital."

I threw up the middle finger. "Fuck you guys."

"Fuck me?" Robbie snapped. "Fuck you. I didn't criticize your choice. I'm for it. Shit. I'll even take a few myself."

"I need new friends."

"You need to straighten out," Ed warned.

"Or join the army," Robbie said.

We all laughed at that one.

The shrooms kicked in. The next thing I knew, I was alone. The TV played Seinfeld on repeat. I stared at screen. An overwhelming shame gripped me. The kind of shame you feel after masturbating for the first time. I am dirty. The people on TV didn't make any sense. It was pathetic. Characters appeared on set for a moment, spouted their scripted lines, the laugh track came on, then they exited stage right. My blood boiled. What the hell was I doing? I nearly died for Christ's sake, and here I was high the morning after. Mushrooms. I hated mushrooms. Why did I take them? Where were my friends?

What kind of friends do I have, giving me shrooms when there's still stickies all over my body? The laughter on TV caused the room to pulse, still, I couldn't pull my eyes from the screen. Each body carefully positioned to look natural. Goddammit. I looked around for the remote. It was on the floor beside my bed. I snagged at it desperately. The room started to cave in. I turned the TV off. Black screen. Maybe that was me. Lights out for good. I closed my eyes. Maybe if I could get some sleep, that would do me good. But closing my eyes didn't help. My memories were shadows. Edgar Allan Poe villains played on the back of my eyelids.

Each of them was me. Jessie. Casey. My mom. Danielle. For what? I tucked my knees to my chest.

Lying fetal, I started to cry. I wanted to scream but nothing came out. I rocked where I lay. It must have been hours. How long do these things take to wear off? I don't want to die. Please, God, don't let me die. I hate mushrooms. I've always hated mushrooms. I'm not going to do mushrooms anymore. I'm not going to do any of it anymore. Never. That's a lie. You're a liar. You destroy everything you touch. You should string yourself up right now. Jump off a chair into oblivion. But Casey, it didn't work for him. Then I'll cut my wrists. Shut up. You don't deserve death. You need to suffer for what you've done. Oh, God, please stop this trip.

Something crept down the stairs. Creak. Pause. Creee-eaak. Pause. Slow walk. One step at a time. I guess that's the only way to do steps. Who's there? I can hear them breath. Someone's standing behind the door.

Bang. Bang. Bang.

"Troy?"

Was that my mother?

"Troy," she said again. "Is everything okay in there?"

"Mom?"

"Troy, I'm coming in."

"Mom! Don't come in!"

She opened the door. Her face grew and filled the space. Her eyes flamed. "What are you on?"

"Nothing Mom, leave me alone. I told you not to come in."

She rushed me. Or so it seemed. She shook my shoulders so hard I thought my neck would break. Or so it seemed. I don't know. She yelled something but I didn't know what. She bawled, too.

Mom pulled me close to her chest and held me. I thought I would suffocate. Fade to black.

I woke up several hours later. I didn't recognize my room. Something about it was off. Things looked rummaged. Books out of line. Remote placed on the TV. Drawers not closed all the way. Did she go through my stuff while I was passed out?

I remembered the envelope on my desk; the grocery bag with the DVDs and mushrooms. The DVDs were on my desk, but the envelope and the grocery bag were missing. I felt for my phone under the sheets. It was missing, too. I leaned off the bed and looked underneath. Not there either.

"What the fuck?"

My head killed. I needed a line, bad.

Upstairs I could hear my mom talking with someone. Not on the phone, in the house. A man's voice. My dad? It couldn't be my dad. Whoever it was, the feeling in my gut told me I was in for it this time.

. . .

He had his back to me. The way his dark grey blazer hugged his shoulders it was either a size too small or he'd just come from the gym. Trim haircut. The man rested his clasped hands on the table. My mom sat in the chair across from him. I thought this odd and then I noticed the envelope in the centre of the table. My envelope.

The man turned around. There was nothing special about his face only I couldn't help think I'd seen him before.

She spoke first, "Troy, this is Detective Roberts."

"You didn't," I said.

He turned around and I was certain I'd seen him before. Why would I know a detective?

He waved his hand over the empty chair. "Have a seat, son."

"What the fuck is this?"

"I just want to ask you a few questions."

"Mom!" I yelled. "What have you done?"

The detective lowered his eyes at me. "We can do this at the station if you want."

I couldn't believe what I was hearing. How could she sell me out like this?

My mom spoke, "Sit down, Troy." And I knew she wasn't messing around. I'd never heard my mom so stern in my entire life.

I thought about bolting out the front door, but then all of a sudden, I felt spun like I had the night before. My heart leapt to my throat. The room faded to black around the edges of my vision. I gasped air. I felt for the wall behind me.

The slap across my face jarred me back to the kitchen. My mom stood stoic.

She dropped her chin. "I'm sorry, Troy," she said.

My mouth gaped.

"This is for the best." She pulled the empty seat from the table. "Now sit down."

"Detective Roberts is the gentlemen who carried you home the night your friend left you in the ditch," she said.

"And you called him?"

"I didn't call him, Troy," she said. "He came by."

I glared at the cop. "So, you just happened to be in the neighbourhood and thought you'd check in on me."

His smile was curt. Cops can be so condescending when they want to be. If my mom wasn't sitting right there, I'd have told him to go fuck himself. Maybe not. I don't know. I didn't like the way he grinned though.

"I wish I had been following up, Troy," he said. "But no, that's not why I'm here."

What did I do now, I thought? What hadn't I done? My eyes darted to envelope between them and I immediately averted them somewhere else. I hoped he didn't see that.

"If I was your parent, I would have called me though. I'd have been terrified you'd end up right in this same situation, or worse."

My mom sighed guiltily. I wanted to hit him. "This is not her fault," I said.

"No, Troy," he said. "It's not. This is on you."

"So, what are you here for then?" I said.

"A call came into the station yesterday," he said. "A rape allegation."

My eyes narrowed. That fucking bitch, I thought. Rape.

"You can imagine my surprise when I learned the name was the same as the young man who I carried home the other night. The same young man who nearly died of a drug overdose. The very same Troy Brinkman sitting right here at this table in front of me."

My eyes could have burned holes in the kitchen wall.

"By the look on your face I'd say you know what I'm talking about."

I didn't say anything.

"Troy," my mom said. "Answer the detective."

I looked at him but didn't say anything.

"Did you rape someone, Troy?" my mom asked.

"I didn't rape anyone, Mom. This is total bullshit."

"Are you telling me you don't know Jessie Bailey?"

"He does," my mom said. "The used to go together every now and again."

I slapped the table. "Are you kidding me? This is a fucking cop. Don't talk to cops. I didn't do anything."

"We're just having a conversation, Troy. Very informal." He relaxed his hands in front of him. I'm sure it was some humanizing technique to get a confession or something. "You and Jessie were something of a couple, yes?"

I washed my hands over my face. If there was ever I time I needed a line, it was now.

"We fuck from time to time."

"If that's the case, what do you think possessed her to call in an accusation as serious as rape, Troy"

They way these two kept using my name in every other sentence really pissed me off.

"Maybe she's on her period–"

"Troy!" my mom gasped.

"We can have this chat, here, with your mom, relaxed and unofficial," he said. "Or if you want to be a smart ass, I can bring you in right now and start playing hardball."

I sucked my lip. Either way I was screwed. I knew it wasn't going to end well.

"Jessie has a boyfriend," I said.

"Yes, Mitch. He came with her to the hospital for the examination."

"Examination?"

"To support the accusation."

I imagined a butch lady cop snapping blue latex gloves over her hands. Her spreading Jessie's legs and fingering the cunt in this rape hunt. I grinned.

"Something funny about all this?" he asked unfeelingly.

I wiped the grin off my face. "It's just absurd," I said. "He probably found out, and she panicked. I mean, that was my first thought when he called me."

"So, you knew what she accused you of?"

"I didn't know for sure. She's a head case." Were we really having this conversation? "And it's not true. I didn't think anything of it."

"The examination showed signs of forced entry," he said. "Tears consistent with those found on victims of this crime."

"I haven't committed a crime. Everything we did was consensual."

"Did you ever get rough with her? Force her into situation where she didn't want to go?"

"What? No."

"Troy," my mom said.

"Mom, I didn't do it. I can't even believe we're having this conversation." I looked back at the detective. "I hope the bitch did get raped for all this bullshit she's causing."

My head snapped forward. Pain shot through my skull and struck the back of my eyes. I saw red. "What the fuck, Mom!"

"I did not raise a son to speak about women like that."

I stared at her, teeth clenched.

"Troy," he said. He wasn't even trying to hide his smugness. "Why don't you tell me what happened."

I rubbed the back of my head. No good. This was no good at all.

He continued. "The problem with these types of calls, without witness, without an examination immediately following the incident, it usually becomes a case of he said she said." He softened his face. He almost looked empathetic. "If you give me your 'he said,' in all likelihood the thing will probably die right here on the table."

I don't know why but I started talking. I told him about moving into the apartment. I told him how Jessie came over and we fucked like we always had, how my friends showed up unannounced, that she got spooked and took off. I didn't tell him about the pills.

"Jessie said something about you giving her Ecstasy?"

She should have known better than to add that detail.

"It wasn't like that," I said.

"But you were on Ecstasy?"

My lugs deflated. "Yeah, we got high. We had crazy sex. When she left, I noticed the sheets were a mess."

"What do you mean a mess?"

Fuck, fuck, fuck.

He tapped his index finger on the table. It sounded like someone at the door.

"Troy," he said. "What do you mean the sheets were a mess?"

"There was some blood."

"Blood?" my mom questioned.

"And you didn't think that maybe something was wrong?"

"I thought she was on her period." I should have never mentioned the blood. What was I thinking? I should know better. Talking to cops.

"The report showed negative for menstruation."

"I didn't rape Jessie. I've never raped anyone. I wouldn't. This is fucked. I have no idea why she made this up. Except for what I already said about Mitch finding out about her and I. What am I supposed to do?"

"Are you a drug addict, Troy?" he said.

My voice cracked, "What?" My face flushed.

"Are you addicted to drugs? Coke, speed, Ecstasy?"

My mom stared in wait.

At least he'd dropped the Jessie business.

"I'm not a junkie."

"But you do a lot of drugs?"

"Everybody my age does."

"You do more than your fair share though, right?"

"I don't know what you're getting at."

"Your mom found this bag in your room." He picked up a grocery bag from beside his chair and set it on the table. It was the bag Robbie left. Mushrooms. An ounce. Maybe more.

"Do you know what's in this bag, Troy?"

"It's not mine."

"I didn't ask you who it belonged to," he said, "I asked if you knew what was in it."

He dumped the bag on the table. A large sandwich bag bursting with dried caps of mushrooms tumbled onto the table and rolled like dice beneath my gaze. I shivered. This was a bad trip. He wanted me to answer the question. I told him I thought they looked like mushrooms. He shook the bag again. Two little baggies fell out.

"And these?" he asked.

It looked like maybe a gram of coke and a couple Blue Starz. Awesome, I thought. Just fucking great.

I didn't say anything.

"Troy."

"Don't you need like a warrant or something to go through my stuff?"

"I gave it to him, Troy," my mom said.

"Your mom invited me in the house."

"I don't know where that stuff came from," I said. "It's not mine."

"Troy, I'm going to be honest with you," he said, "things are not looking good."

"No shit."

"I came over to check on the domestic issue, and do you know what I found?"

"My son high out of his mind," my mom said in fluctuating tones. "Two days after he nearly died."

"Your mother in tears. This bag of drugs," he said. "Then there's this envelope stuffed to the seams with another indictable offence."

I knew I was screwed. Deny, deny, deny, act surprised, offer to help. Somehow, I didn't think choosing the boldest way out was going to help me this time. Besides. I could never snitch on Robbie. Not in a million years. Even if this was all his fault.

"Do you want to tell me about what's in this envelope, Troy?"

"I thought you said it was another indictable offence?"

"What it looks like to me is possession with intent to distribute."

I could hear the judge's gavel slamming a cell door closed behind me. I couldn't go to prison. Not over this.

"If you're an addict," he continued. "A lawyer might be able to plea you down, being your first offence and all. If you agree to rehab–"

"So much for a friendly conversation," I said.

"Troy," he said. "I'm just trying to help."

"Yeah," I said. "Of course, you are."

He turned to my mother. "I'm sorry Mrs. Brinkman, but I'm going to have to place your son under arrest."

"I understand."

"Mom!"

I stared at her for an answer, but one didn't come. My forehead fell to the table. I interlaced my fingers on top.

"Troy Brinkman," he said, voice monotone. "I'm arresting you for—" And I knew the rest. You have the right to retain and instruct counsel without delay, blah, blah, blah. Talk about a bad trip. He clinked the bracelets around my wrist and led me out the front door.

I thought my mom would be telling me how this was for the best, how she'd come to all the court dates and visit weekly. I thought she'd say something comforting, but she didn't. She just stood at the top of the steps with arms crossed, a defeated frown on her face.

What got me though was Danielle being there.

As the detective walked me down the steps and toward the back seat of his unmarked, black, whatever vehicle it was, she walked toward the house. Mom must have called her before all this detective crap happened.

Danielle's mouth lopped ajar ever so slight; her head craned to follow mine as we crossed paths. She didn't say a word. She just walked. Like the detective and I just drove away. Like the entire ride had just happened.

CPSIA information can be obtained
at www.ICGtesting.com
Printed in the USA
LVHW051343070623
748724LV00001B/2